"Travis, watch out!"

Lily's warning came soon er   .. wasn't
knocked out by what would've been a full hit to the
head.

The attacker hesitated and Lily told Timber to attack.
This time, the attacker seemed to have had enough,
because he stood and ran for the door, kicking behind
him and connecting with Timber hard enough that the
dog yelped.

"Timber!" Lily hurried toward her, but the pain in her
side made her double over. Nothing had ever hurt like
this. The dog was already up and sprinting after the
man. Was he seriously going to get away *again*?

"Timber!" she yelled again, but the K-9 ignored her,
driven, it seemed, by a desire stronger than the one
she usually had to please Lily.

"Lily, stop!" Travis called. "Don't go after him. It's not
worth it."

She knew he was right, but the attacker had
threatened her life more than once. Next time, he'd
probably do worse damage.

She had a feeling today had been a warning.

Sarah Varland lives in Alaska with her husband, John, their two boys and their dogs. Her passion for books comes from her mom; her love for suspense comes from her dad, who has spent a career in law enforcement. When she's not writing, she's often found dog mushing, hiking, reading, kayaking, drinking coffee or enjoying other Alaskan adventures with her family.

Books by Sarah Varland

Love Inspired Suspense

Treasure Point Secrets
Tundra Threat
Cold Case Witness
Silent Night Shadows
Perilous Homecoming
Mountain Refuge
Alaskan Hideout
Alaskan Ambush
Alaskan Christmas Cold Case
Alaska Secrets
Alaskan Mountain Attack
Alaskan Mountain Search
Alaskan Wilderness Rescue
K-9 Alaskan Defense

Visit the Author Profile page at LoveInspired.com.

K-9 ALASKAN DEFENSE

SARAH VARLAND

LOVE INSPIRED SUSPENSE
INSPIRATIONAL ROMANCE

 LOVE INSPIRED® SUSPENSE
INSPIRATIONAL ROMANCE

ISBN-13: 978-1-335-48400-0

K-9 Alaskan Defense

Copyright © 2025 by Sarah Varland

Love Inspired
22 Adelaide St. West, 41st Floor
Toronto, Ontario M5H 4E3, Canada
www.LoveInspired.com

Printed in U.S.A.

Now unto him that is able to do exceedingly abundantly above all that we ask or think, according to the power that worketh in us, unto him be glory in the church by Christ Jesus throughout all ages, world without end. Amen.

—*Ephesians* 3:20–21

To my family, who has faithfully supported every dream I've ever had. I'm so blessed. And to God, whose dreams are even better and bigger than my own.

ONE

No matter how fast Lily Peterson ran, it was never quite fast enough. Her feet dug into the soft dirt of the Alaskan mountain side trail, winding along the ridgeline. The view in front of her was a study in contrasts, wilderness that gradually gave way to houses, then the city of Anchorage ahead in the distance. So many buildings. So many lights.

She loved the beauty of it from up here, running with her German shepherd, Timber, but she was thankful to live twenty miles north of the city. The town of Silvertip Creek, named for the brown bears who frequented the area, offered her the solitude of the wilderness that she needed. Especially after everything that had happened this past year.

Her pace quickened inadvertently, and Lily felt the welcome burn in her muscles that always came when she pushed herself. Timber kept pace, like she always did. Lily couldn't have asked for a more faithful companion, even though Timber really had never been meant for her...

She took a deep breath, tried to clear her mind, and ran faster and faster until she finally had to stop for air. Timber stopped beside her, and Lily reached down and petted her in between gasps.

"Good dog." With a long inhale, she began to stretch, looking out at the view where Cook Inlet met the rocky shore. In the land of the midnight sun, there would be light for hours yet since it was only eight o'clock at night. But she and

Timber both needed dinner, so it was time to head back.

"Ready to go home?" she asked, expecting the dog's ears to perk like they usually did at the word. For a German shepherd who'd been trained as a police dog, Timber was quite a fan of relaxing on the couch and generally staying close to home. These mountain trips were more for Lily than Timber, though she had a feeling the dog viewed it as her duty to take Lily for runs.

This time, though, Timber continued to stare off into the distance, farther down the jagged ridgeline, past any real trail. There was a look of focus in her eyes Lily had never seen before.

She felt her own breathing slow as she listened. Her heart still pounding, she leaned closer to Timber, trying to see what the dog saw.

Everything seemed to her to be the same as it had been moments before, but Timber was clearly picking up on something Lily wasn't. It shouldn't be surprising—the dog had been born, bred and trained to work. Until an attack a year ago had nearly taken her life and left her with an injury that led to her early retirement. She'd been sent to live with Lily, as a sort of condolence for the fact that Timber's handler, Lily's fiancé, hadn't survived.

"What is it, girl?"

Timber whined, shifting uncomfortably. Lily's shoulders tensed, and slowly she started to reach for Timber's collar. The dog usually hiked off leash, but she was behaving strangely. There could be a moose, a bear…

Timber took off at a full sprint.

"Timber, no!" Lily leapt to her feet and took off after her. Muscles that had been so glad to get a break began burning anew with the sudden increase in activity. "Timber!"

The German shepherd ignored her, something that would have been unthinkable moments before. Timber's recall was bombproof—a remnant of her former job. Lily had never had trouble with her before. This was terrifyingly out of character.

Lily picked her way farther down the ridgeline, unable to run in some places where the trail hugged the side of the mountain or where jagged rocks jutted out. How Timber hadn't lost her footing, Lily didn't know. The dog was extremely athletic and in good shape, but her back leg had never been quite the same after she'd been shot.

She kept her eyes on Timber as long as she could, praying she'd be okay, but then Timber leapt over a rock and out of sight. Lily bit back her scream to avoid startling the dog even more and hurried after her.

She noticed the smell first, dense and

reminiscent of iron. Reddish brown blood soaked the mountainside foliage, staining the ground around the body of a motionless man.

Timber sat beside him, whining and pawing the ground. If Matt had told Lily details about Timber's training, Lily couldn't remember them. It seemed to her as though the dog had found the person. Or...the body? Was Timber trained to do that?

Willing herself to keep it together, Lily started forward. Only to be knocked sideways by a blurry force.

She screamed as she slid down the scree on the mountainside, her hands fighting for something to grab, anything that would keep her from plummeting farther. Out of the corner of her eye, she could see the drop—it was much too far to fall and survive. She twisted her body to fall back onto the ridge, looking around wildly to figure out what had hit her.

A figure crouched nearby—a man, she guessed by the size and build—wearing black sweats, a black hoodie and a black ski mask over his face. He was reaching for her, rough hands grabbing her wrists, when Timber growled and launching herself at the man.

She couldn't lose Timber, not with all the other things she'd lost in the past year. She also knew she couldn't fight off this man alone. He was too big, too strong, and she'd already almost fallen. Even with adrenaline coursing through her veins, Lily wasn't sure she could sustain another attack.

Timber bit down, and the man released Lily, his scream ripping the air. Every muscle in Lily's body tensed, and panic tightened her throat. She hurried out of arms reach, toward the body Timber had found, trying not to think about the gruesome scene behind her. Instead, she watched as Timber let go of the man's arm and jumped at him again, growling.

The man kicked at her, but Timber clamped down on his other arm. He threw her off violently, and Lily watched in horror as Timber flew toward the knife-edge of the ridgeline. She ran to her, heart in her throat, as the dog fell just inches away from the drop-off.

With Lily's eyes off her attacker, the man turned to run away. Timber's body tensed to chase after the man, but Lily left no room for argument in her tone. "Stop, no."

Timber stayed. Lily waited, crouched at her side, until she could no longer hear the man's feet crashing through the brush.

The danger had passed, at least for now, but her heart still pounded in her chest. Why had the man attacked her, whoever he was? Why had he hurt the man behind her?

Was he even still alive? She had to check.

Moving slowly, she approached him carefully and knelt down beside him. His eyes were closed. She glanced along the rest of his body, then looked immediately away. He had to be dead. No one could lose this much blood and not be... She felt for a pulse at the man's wrists and waited.

Nothing.

She moved her hands to his neck.

Still nothing.

Exhaling, she felt defeat press against her, hating the idea that she'd been unable to help. She stepped away from the body and threw up the little lunch she'd eaten earlier. When she finally managed to get her nausea under control, she pulled out her phone and dialed 911 to report what she'd found. Talk about

another layer of trauma—police officers were the last people she wanted to
talk to today. A memory flashed in her
mind, a police car in her driveway, a
knock at her door.

Lily took a slow, deep breath. Held it.
Let it out.

She couldn't do this. She absolutely
couldn't face the police alone. Not today.
She glanced back down at her phone.
But did she dare not? There was no one
else to call. Heart still pounding, Lily
scrolled through her contacts, finger
hovering over the one number she never
thought she'd have a reason to call again.

Travis Beckett had broken her heart
years ago, and she'd been less than
thrilled when she discovered he was
her fiancé's partner at the Anchorage
Police Department. Having him back in
her life in any capacity was something
she didn't want.

But she didn't know anyone else connected to law enforcement who might be able to brace her for the storm she was afraid was coming. A man had died, the violent wounds puncturing his body speaking of rage. Intention.

A criminal was out there right now, loose. He could come back any minute.

Refusing to overthink it anymore, she pressed the screen. Waited. "Travis… It's Lily. I need you."

Hearing from Lily Peterson wasn't something Travis would have expected to happen in this lifetime. Their last link had been broken when Matt died. But he'd recognize her voice anywhere, had known it was her as soon as she said his name, though he hadn't had her number saved in his phone, and then she'd said she needed him…

The protective feeling that welled in him surprised him. She hadn't finished explaining by the time he grabbed his keys and started for his truck.

She was far up the ridgeline of Avalanche Peak, but he still had his trail runners on from the short run he'd taken after work. He guessed police officers probably brought up bad memories for her; the last time she'd been around many of them, she'd been hearing the details of her fiancé's death. He'd call them when he'd reached Lily, to make sure she didn't have to talk to them alone.

The trail was hard beneath his feet as he ran to the location she'd described. Finally the smell hit him. Blood.

And a body. Nothing she'd said could have prepped him for the sight of that much blood on the ground. Lily knelt beside the man, sobbing into her hands. Timber was pressing against her as though for reassurance.

He'd missed that dog. The department

had offered her to Travis after Matt died and Timber's injury forced her into early retirement, but he hadn't felt right about taking her. Not when Lily was alone, her future decimated by one person's bad choices, her fiancé in the wrong place at the wrong time.

Travis should have been the one in the line of fire. He'd been a second too slow. Now he was alive, and Matt was dead, and Travis had wrecked Lily's life... again.

How was she? He'd wondered many times over the past year since the shooting. One year ago today. He'd finished out the next few months after that with the Anchorage Police Department and then resigned, moved from his apartment in the city back to Silvertip Creek, where he'd lived growing up. He was helping his brother at his hardware store while he tried to figure out what he wanted to do with his life. All Travis knew for sure was that he was ready for a job that involved fewer homicides and drug cases and more small-town things.

His days were slower now. Easier.

Still too much time to think, but there wasn't much a job could do about that. One of these days that was probably an issue Travis was going to have to solve himself.

"Lily, you okay?" A stupid question, he decided as soon as it left his mouth.

Her pale blue eyes were red rimmed from crying. She blinked but didn't answer him.

"How's he?" He nodded toward the body on the ground.

"I think… I think he's dead."

"And Timber?"

Lily turned to the dog and scratched around her ears. Travis thought he saw the tenseness in her shoulders soften. Good, that had been part of the idea with Lily adopting Timber.

"She seems okay. She found him. Completely ignored me when I called her back, just took off, and then I found her here." Her face was wrinkled into a frown. "Is that, you know, normal? Like is that something she's trained to do?"

"Possibly." He didn't know the degree to which he should go into Timber's training with Lily. She was trained for search and rescue and was able to sniff out narcotics, contact a suspect on command and deliver a bite, among other things. She'd been an incredibly promising police canine, only three when she'd been shot, which was a shame.

So much about that incident was.

"Did you notice anything else here? Anyone else, evidence that says someone else was here?"

She hesitated. His stomach tightened.

"Someone attacked me."

It was like someone had hit him square in the chest. He fought to catch his breath and breathe normally again. "Tell me what happened."

She did so, detailing the attacker's large build, his scream, Timber's attack and his retreat.

"You're okay?" He stepped closer to her, scanning her for signs of injury.

She held out her arm. "Bruises, but I think that's all."

The harsh purple of the bruises against her light skin made him want to find the guy himself.

"Why were you way up here, past the regular trail?" He tried to keep the judgment and frustration out of his tone. The idea of Lily taking chances like this grated at him. She was supposed to be in her coffee shop in Silvertip Creek, where it was safe, not on mountainsides risking her life discovering dead men.

Even as he thought it, he realized his error. Lily was free to do what she wanted. Always had been. She'd made that clear when they were both in high school, when they'd been dating for over a year and graduation had been approaching, and Travis had thought their futures might be together...

Forget what he thought. He'd been wrong.

He looked at Lily, who was watching him. Dang it, he'd never been able to hide his thoughts from her. If he wasn't imagining it, her face had softened slightly, when she should have been defensive at his unreasonable question. Could she still sense his lingering feelings for her, whatever they were? Not romantic feelings, certainly, but caring? Too much caring for someone who was essentially a stranger now.

"Timber needed a run."

"There are other trails." Travis said. His eyes were drawn back to the body and a familiar clenching feeling tightened in his stomach.

He'd seen bodies like this too many times, was altogether too aware of the ways people hurt each other. It was why he'd left police work after the death of his partner. He'd tried to stick with it for a couple of months, went to the counseling the department had mandated, but none of it seemed to work. He despised the job he'd once enjoyed, and there didn't seem to be anything he could do that would change that. So he left, joined his brother in the hardware store business and avoided reminders of what his life had once been like.

Today was a jarring reminder, in so many ways. Lily's pale face. A situation that felt impossible. The tension as they realized someone would not make it out alive. Just like last year.

"Travis." Lily's voice was tense.

He whirled to face her. She'd walked back to the ridgeline where the dead man had been. She was staring at a tiny piece of paper on the ground, stark white against the brown of the blood-soaked earth, immediately beside the body, against his hip like it had dislodged from a pocket.

"He dropped something. Could that matter?"

"For what?"

"Finding out more about who he is, why he was attacked…"

"That's the police's job."

"But you're…"

"I'm not anymore."

"Oh." She stopped, looked away from the paper and up at him. "Since when?"

"Not long after."

She nodded. She clearly knew what he meant. For once in their lives, they probably understood what the other was feeling better than anyone else. Lily and Matt had been engaged for months before he was killed. Travis had been his partner at work, handling Timber together, investigating together... Each of them had lost a chunk of themselves when they'd lost Matt.

He saw emotions chase across Lily's face as she seemed to realize that, too. Again, he watched her face soften.

"You asked me why I was up here," she said.

"Yes."

She shook her head, and he thought he caught a flash of disappointment in her eyes. "Don't you know what day it is? It's one year since he died." She reached out a hand and pointed. "See that spot on the mudflats right there?"

He did. And suddenly he understood why she'd ventured onto this ridgeline. From anywhere else, the view of that place was blocked. But from here?

She could see the place where Matt had drowned in the relentless Alaskan tide and her dreams for the future had been lost forever.

TWO

Lily almost couldn't believe she'd pointed that out to Travis, the place where Matt had died, or that they were talking about this thing that she didn't talk about with anyone so casually. But Travis probably understood how she felt better than most people would. He didn't understand losing a loved one, of course...

She slammed the door on that thought almost as soon as she'd opened it. Technically speaking, maybe he did know what that was like. Not losing to death, perhaps, but maybe to the other person's choices.

"The counselor I was seeing told me I

had to figure out a way that worked for me to mark the days, whether that was to do something special or just somehow remember him." She shrugged.

"I think that sounds wise."

A minute of silence passed, and then Travis shifted beside her, and she felt his glance on her. He wanted to ask or say something, she was fairly certain. Finally she looked his direction. "What is it?"

"Hmm?"

"What's on your mind? You seem preoccupied and not with…" She didn't have the energy to talk about it, so she motioned with her hand instead. "This."

"It's you."

She turned to him. Waited in a heavy silence as their eyes met. Her heartbeat quickened ever so slightly.

"I'm worried about you," he clarified. "You said the guy attacked you."

"Oh." She shook her head, scattering

thoughts of the past. "Not badly. I mean, I'm okay. Bruised, but…" She trailed off, looked down at her arms.

Travis moved closer, and his fingers brushed against her arm as he reached to look closer. Just as quickly, the contact was broken as he snatched his hand away.

"May I?" he asked.

She nodded and held her arms out to him.

There was no reason for her to react this way to Travis's touch. However, while any romance between them had ended years ago and badly, it appeared she hadn't entirely forgotten the connection they'd once had. Goose bumps chased down her arms.

"I hate that you're hurt. Maybe you should get these looked at?"

Already, she was shaking her head.

"At least clean the cuts well. It looks

like you got scraped." He motioned to a spot on her forearm.

Lily glanced at it. "Probably from when I fell."

"You fell up there?"

"Yeah, when we were struggling, before Timber fought him off."

Timber seemed to almost material-ize beside her, and Lily smiled as she reached down, scratched the dog be-tween her ears. When she looked up again, Travis was staring down the sheer drop-off along the ridgeline.

Lily looked away. She didn't want to think about what could have so easily happened.

He took a deep breath and turned back to her. Apparently he didn't want to think about it, either. "So this paper." Travis walked over to where it lay, and Lily followed. The corners of the paper were edged in deep brown, as though it had soaked up some of the blood.

"From his pocket, you think?" she suggested.

"Best I can guess. Hardly anyone hikes back here." He nudged it with a foot.

"I've got some thin gloves in my backpack. I could pick it up with those?"

"Better than nothing. I'll do it, though."

She slung the small runner's pack off her back and dug out the gloves, then handed them to Travis. The gray gloves lined with hot pink fleece looked funny stretched across his hands. She watched as he bent and picked up the folded paper carefully. There was a torn piece of scotch tape on the back side of it, dirtied by the ground, its stickiness long gone.

Travis stood beside her as he unfolded it. The words written in black ink stood out against the white of the paper.

742 Aspen

Her heart skipped.

It had been almost a year since Lily had experienced what she was feeling right now. Her chest felt tight. Tighter. Tighter. It was a normal fear reaction, she tried to remind herself even as her world seemed to narrow. *Breathe in. Breathe out.*

She glanced at Travis, but his world seemed unshaken. He was frowning but in confusion. "Why would…" he started, but she interrupted.

"It's my address."

If he'd been glad before that Lily had called him, he was extra thankful now. His mind raced. Why was her address on this paper? Who was the dead man she'd found in the wilderness? Was she meant to have found him, was it some kind of trap? Regardless, the body had some connection to Lily.

The wilderness around them no longer

held its usual benign feeling, but rather one of threat. Even the clouds looked darker to his mind now.

The danger had just increased past his comfort level.

"We need to get out of here. I'll call the police on our way down so they can come for the body, and I'll swing by the station to give them the note. I don't want to leave it in case the killer comes back for it."

"No, the tape. What was taped to the letter?"

She was right, the tape. Better to investigate that now than wonder later... Investigate? What was he thinking? He was a former cop, emphasis on *former*, and she owned a coffee shop. Neither of them had any business investigating anything.

Except Travis wasn't comfortable leaving her safety to the police, no matter how competent they were. He knew how busy police departments got. There was a chance a case like this could get set aside once progress on it stalled, and he couldn't afford for Lily to be in danger during the interim.

"We can look for a few minutes and then we're out of here. This might be some kind of trap."

"Don't you think I'd be dead or hurt worse or something by now if it was?"

Travis didn't answer. He was already crouching to look at the ground. He'd shoved the paper with the address into his back pocket. Probably there weren't any usable prints on it, but you never knew for sure.

Out of the corner of his eye, he saw Lily bend down to search, too. Timber still sat near her, watching.

Man, he loved that dog. She was one of the best he'd ever worked with or had the pleasure to watch work. On one hand, it was a shame she'd had to retire early because of her injury, but on the other, he was glad she was with Lily.

"I found a key." Her voice sounded strangled.

"Are you okay?"

He watched as she swallowed hard and shook her head slightly. "No. I mean, yes, I will be, but…"

"Let's get off the mountain. Now."

A wind picked up and chilled the air as they hurried back across the ridgeline. Travis felt his heart in his throat every time he watched Lily traverse one of the knifelike edges carefully, arms out to grab on to something in case of a fall.

Finally they were back on the main trail. Almost without thinking, he looked out toward the inlet. Sure enough, he couldn't see the spot where Matt had died from here. But how had Lily known there would be a view of it?

He asked her as much, partially out of curiosity and partially to give them something to talk about to make the time go faster until she was safely away from this place. As far away as he could convince her to get.

"Matt and I used to come up here. You know he loved trail running."

Travis nodded. He'd never seen why someone would want to run up in the mountains when he could walk, take in the view, really be present and enjoy the moment, but he knew his friend had loved it.

"He took me up here once, not long before he died actually, and I just remembered the view."

"But you don't go on that trail often, right?" He feared for her safety if she did, and was also concerned if her movements were predictable. Could someone have assumed that she'd find the dead man?

"I don't. I haven't been back since."

Travis nodded. They continued picking their way down the trail, which angled toward the base of the mountain. His car was parked at the trailhead, and he assumed Lily's was, too, though he'd only noticed a couple other cars in the lot. The trailhead led to several different places and was fairly popular, but it was a chilly day even for Alaskan summer, so not as many people were out.

"Where's your car?" he asked.

"I walked."

He didn't know that there was anything to say to that. It was completely reasonable that she'd have walked here a few hours ago. But now, with what had changed… Why did a dead man have her address? Was she in more or less danger now because he was dead?

And why—his mind finally wrapped itself around asking—why had the dead man looked familiar? Something chased around on the edges of his mind, the shadows of a cobwebby idea. He'd have to get back to that later.

"How far is it to your house?"

"Less than a mile."

"Is there anywhere else you could go for now?"

She raised her eyebrows and said nothing. It was answer enough.

"Listen, I know I don't have a right to tell you what to do anymore."

"Never did, actually."

"Right, but..."

"Could we talk about this at my house?"

"Fine. Lead on." He blew out a breath of frustration that he knew wasn't fair to direct toward Lily.

This was a situation he never could have imagined finding himself in, being back in Lily's life in any capacity. He struggled to wrap his mind around all the implications of it as he followed her down the narrow trail. She followed Timber, whose body language didn't seem to indicate any particular threats at the moment. Travis had been watching her for a while for any signs that there was something particular to be concerned about.

"Here it is, just up here…" Lily turned off the main trail onto a much less traveled trail. Travis had known there were a few houses up here on the edge of town, up against the mountains, but hadn't known Lily was one of them. She rounded the corner. Stopped.

The tiny cabin in the clearing was cozy, welcoming, exactly what he would have pictured her in.

It was also on fire.

Timber whined and shifted uncomfortably.

"Timber, stay!" Lily yelled and then sprinted toward the log cabin and the flames.

"Lily, no!" Travis shouted and chased

after her until he lost sight of her in the smoke and flames.

She was gone.

Her house. Her books. Her photos—why couldn't she just keep them on her computer like other people her age? Her coffee mugs from places she'd visited. Her favorite rug. She thought of all of them as she sprinted up the hill into the clearing where her house was in flames.

Mind somehow still working, she pulled her phone out of her pocket and dialed 911. "My house is on fire! Help!"

"I'll get someone there as soon as I can. What's your address?" The calm, neutral voice of the dispatcher almost made her angry and more panicked. This was urgent, didn't she know that? Of course Lily realized it was their job to sound like that. Maybe it steadied some people. It did nothing for her.

"742 Aspen," she said as fast as she

could, then hung up, despite the woman's insistence she stay on the call. She had to do something. Her house was on fire.

The hose was on the side of the house opposite most of the fire. Of course sometimes fire could be in the walls—she'd probably read it in a book somewhere, but the random fact chose now to present itself in her mind. If she hurried, could she put the fire out by herself?

She heard Travis yelling. Of course he wouldn't want her to fight the fire herself. But it wasn't his house.

"Lily, stop."

"No."

"They're just things." He reached for her arm, and she shrugged away from him.

"I said no! It's all I have, Travis. I won't lose my house. I won't."

With a quick glance backward to make sure Timber was staying put—she was, though the look on her face made it clear this wasn't her preference—Lily grabbed the hose and started to fight.

At first, the steam rising was her only result, and the effort seemed pointless. Then finally she thought she saw the flames lessening. They hadn't gotten to the roof yet, as if content to feed on the hand-hewn log walls. Little by little the fire retreated, until Lily heard the sirens approaching. At that point, she gladly stepped back and let the professionals take over.

She called Timber to her side and watched as the Silvertip Creek Fire Department fought to finish saving her little cabin. At some point, Travis came and stood on the other side of her from Timber. Somehow his presence made everything a little better.

When the last of the smoke was extinguished, one of the firefighters walked toward her. He removed his face mask and nodded in her direction. "You're the homeowner?"

Well, she had been. "Yes. Lily Peterson."

"I think we've got it out at this point. It's possible there could still be hot spots. We're going to walk around and make sure that it's out. Once we've confirmed it's safe enough, you can get a few belongings out of the house, but you won't be able to stay here for a few days."

She felt her face scrunch into a frown, and the fireman noticed. "The chemicals. Fires release them, you know."

She hadn't known. "But..." She felt Travis's hand on her arm and stopped. Nodded. "Thank you."

"You did a great job with the hose. Probably saved the house, to be honest. We just finished up what you started."

Lily tried to smile but only managed a sort of half smile as the firefighter walked away.

Was the fire entirely unrelated to finding the dead man? On one hand, it seemed too coincidental that two things with so much gravity and drama could happen in one day. On the other...how could they possibly be related? She didn't know who the man was, she'd found him entirely by accident.

And the fire?

"Will they be able to tell how the fire started?" she asked Travis. Maybe he'd had experiences with fire investigations as a police officer.

"To a degree, yes. They'll know if there was an accelerant that helped the fire spread, or if it was intentional or because of bad wiring..."

"Why would someone do this? I really don't understand. Is it related to the paper with my address?"

Travis shook his head. "I just don't know."

Neither did she. That was the problem.

The firefighter called her over to the house. The door of the cabin was intact, though it had been sprayed down. He eased it open for her and motioned her inside. In a fog, she went through.

The entryway was normal, though she could smell the smoke. The farther she went inside, the more damage she could see. Some of the walls were charred even on the inside. It appeared that over-all the structure was intact, though.

"It all looks pretty good except this back corner." The firefighter motioned to the room that had been her study.

Oh, not her study. Her books…

She did her best to brace herself as they eased the door open.

It was better than it could have been. That's what she kept repeating to her-self over and over. By her side, Timber seemed to tense up, probably mirror-ing Lily's own anxiety. The dog whined, and Lily reached down to pet her for re-assurance.

The bookcase that was built into the outside wall was completely destroyed. It wasn't entirely burned up, but the damage was likely irreparable.

"This room is the reason you're going to need to let the house air out for a couple of days before you try to move back in."

Lily nodded, ran her hands along the spines of some of the books that hadn't been damaged. She looked up. The ceiling had some holes.

"My roof…" She trailed off. "Is it still intact?"

"From the outside it looked okay but you should have it checked out thoroughly by a contractor. I can give you the number of a guy I've seen do wonders with restorations like this."

She nodded. What else was there to do?

Her safe in the corner appeared to

have taken some damage, too, but it was fireproof. She opened it, confirmed that her documents and other things she kept in it were unharmed, then shut it again.

"Matt helped with this room," she mumbled under her breath.

"What was that?" the firefighter asked.

"Nothing," Lily said, unwilling to repeat herself or explain. One year without him, and now…all of these things were happening. It couldn't be a coincidence. A chill ran down her back. Was she in some kind of danger?

She hurried to gather what she wanted for the night, necessities like spare clothes, pj's and toothpaste, but also the book she'd been in the middle of reading, some snacks, and a notebook and pen.

When she got back outside, Travis was still standing in the yard, waiting. Not that she expected him to have gone anywhere. He'd made it quite clear he was taking some kind of protective role, or trying to. The question was, did she want that?

"You okay?" he asked when she stepped outside.

"I have no idea."

"Want to come to my house? I've got a small cabin on my property that I usually rent out to tourists in the summer but it's empty for the next couple of weeks. You could stay in it until you're allowed back in yours? I can plug the address into your phone if you want."

She ran through her other options. Her best friend, Terina, was out of town. She could probably stay there, but it would involve pet sitting for Terina's tiny Chihuahuas, since she'd be displacing the pet sitter. While Timber was well enough behaved, as a rule she didn't seem to enjoy time spent with the smaller dogs biting at her ankles.

"I appreciate that," she said at last. "I'll meet you there?"

"Sure. And, Lily?"

She turned around, met his eyes.

"Be careful."

She felt the weight of his gaze even more than his words. In that moment, Lily realized that she hadn't overreacted. She hadn't been wrong to somehow link the events of this day together: the one-year anniversary of Matt's death; the discovery of the dead man; her burned cabin.

She was in danger for some reason. And with no idea where the danger was coming from, she would have to be alert to all possible sources of trouble if she had any hope of keeping herself safe.

THREE

Travis had just climbed into his car when he saw the Silvertip Police Department patrol car pull into Lily's driveway. An officer who looked vaguely familiar slid out of one them. She was probably in her midthirties, with reddish hair.

Travis put his own car back into Park and got out, walking over to join her. He stuck out a hand to introduce himself. "Travis Beckett."

"You were at APD for a while, right?"

So she had looked familiar. He raised an eyebrow, prompting her for more information.

"I'm Officer Keller. Emily Keller. Zach Keller who works at APD is my brother."

Travis nodded. "Of course, makes sense. Nice to meet you." He could see the resemblance now. He hadn't thought about Zach in months, though the two of them had been close once. Maybe that was a possibility for keeping close to the investigation—it wasn't uncommon for police officers to keep each other posted. He was still technically post certified, so it wouldn't be any kind of violation.

"I'd like to ask Lily Peterson about what happened," Officer Keller went on. "It looks like the report is still pending in the system, but she called 911 earlier today on a ridgeline and found a body is my basic understanding?"

"I'm Lily Peterson." Lily walked up from where she'd been packing her car. She gave Keller a bit more information, then reached into her pocket, with a glance at Travis.

He nodded slightly, in case she was asking his opinion on sharing the note with the police. Anything would help, and the police needed to know everything they knew if there was going to be any kind of hope of solving this case.

"We found this at the scene." Lily handed Officer Keller the note and waited while she looked at it.

"That's this address. Your address."

"Exactly. And there's more." Lily handed the officer the key she'd found. They'd put it into a small plastic bag Lily had in her pack. "I don't know if you guys can get fingerprints off things this small…"

"You'd be amazed at what we can get prints off of."

"Well, I hope it helps. I don't want…" Lily trailed off, not seeming able to articulate more about how she felt.

"We don't want this to drag on. It's disconcerting," Travis finished, glancing at Lily who seemed to give him a small smile of approval.

"As you know," Officer Keller addressed Travis, "we can't promise anything in an investigation. Our latent print department, along with the rest of our tiny crime scene team, is pretty swamped, and the state crime lab is backlogged also. It may be a while before we get anything definitive from these."

Lily nodded. "Thank you, though, for looking into this."

"You're welcome. Anything else happens, call me or Officer Wilkins. He's the one up on the mountain right now recovering the body."

Officer Keller handed Lily a business card, then walked back to her car and drove away.

"You okay?" Travis looked over at Lily.

"Exhausted. I'm just exhausted."

"Let's head to my house. I'll feed you."

It was all he needed to say. She hurried to her car, and Travis did the same.

As he drove the five miles to his house, which was on the other side of Silver-tip Creek from Lily's cabin, Travis went through the facts as he knew them. It was a habit he'd developed in his law enforcement days, a way to process through events.

First, Lily had called him, in trouble because Timber had run off and found a man who was dead. He needed to look into what degree had Timber alerted; how much had she performed according to her search-and-rescue training? K-9s were interesting—you could train them, but they were still living creatures with their own minds. They had some of their own decision-making skills, which some departments let dogs use more than others. It may not be relevant to this case, but he still wanted to know what had really happened to the best of his ability.

Second, someone had set Lily's house on fire. Did they intend to destroy it?

Destroy something inside the house? Hurt or kill her? Scare her? Motives were too varied for him to make any kind of guess.

Third, this was the one-year anniversary of Matt Davis's death. Was that related? Coincidence? Travis didn't believe in coincidences.

Ironic that he wished his friend was here to bounce ideas off of. Matt had always been smart, incredibly so. He didn't come across as an intellectual by any means, but he had a mind for puzzles and if anything qualified, this did.

Of course, if Matt were alive, things might be different. He and Lily would have been married by now, for one thing.

There was something Travis didn't want to think about. The idea of Lily as another man's wife made his stomach feel hollow in a way he wished he could ignore. Surely after all these years he was over her. Wasn't he?

He pulled into his driveway and tried to see his house like she would. How much did she think about the past? Would she imagine what life would have been like if they'd stayed together?

He certainly wouldn't have imagined himself in the house he had now, in a quiet mountainside neighborhood, downright quaint with its weathered logs and A-frame structure. But Matt's death had changed Travis's priorities, as well as his dreams about the future. It had changed him.

He doubted Lily ever gave him much thought at all. It had been years, he reminded himself, and she'd been engaged since then. A real engagement with a real ring and a wedding date, not a class ring and some sincere but flimsy promises.

Climbing out of his car, he did his best to put the past back in his memory where it belonged. In the very back of his mind. She'd called him today as a friend. He had no business getting caught up in the land of what-if and risking that trust. What she needed now was a friend, someone to talk to, someone who would feed her, like he'd promised.

He waited in the driveway until Lily's car pulled in, and then he ushered her inside of his house, making sure to lock the door behind them.

"This is it." He shrugged.

"Wow."

If he'd imagined how she would react, instead of just wondered, he wouldn't have pictured her utterly delighted wide-eyed stare. "Your house is beautiful. It's so peaceful here."

"Thanks." He smiled, remembering every day he'd spent remodeling the house, ripping out old carpet and refinishing long-forgotten hardwood floors. His goal had been to blend the inside of his house with the outside, making it fade into the forest in a way. Having Lily notice and appreciate it warmed a part of himself he hadn't realized was cold.

"Want the grand tour first or dinner?"

Her stomach growled, and she looked down, embarrassed for half a second, and then she looked back up at him with a smile. "Dinner, apparently. Thanks."

They headed to the kitchen, where she ran her hands appreciatively over the countertop. "Nice."

"It's functional."

"Oh, come on, it's so much more than that."

Travis shrugged. "I wanted it to be more than that."

"Well, you succeeded. You really did."

Something in her voice caught his attention, and he looked at her, their eyes meeting and holding for one second. Two.

He looked away first. She was hurting, he reminded himself. She needed a friend. Food. Not some boyfriend from her past confusing her when her life was in chaos already.

"How does beef stew sound?"

"Perfect. Want me to make something? Biscuits maybe? Do you have milk and flour?"

He motioned to the fridge and pantry. "Be my guest."

They worked side by side, the rhythm feeling more natural than it should have as they danced back and forth between counters and pantries and stove.

"That smells so good." Lily said with an appreciative sigh.

"Thanks."

Before long, they were sitting down at the table to eat. "Mind if I pray?" Travis asked.

"Go ahead." Lily replied, but there was something in her voice he couldn't quite identify. Matt had never been much for praying, or faith for that matter. Had that rubbed off on Lily or was he reading too much into her reaction? Hard to say.

After they prayed, they started to eat.

Lily paused. Closed her eyes. "This is so good."

"Self-defense. It was either learn to cook or starve."

She laughed, and he'd forgotten how much the liked the sound. "Well, you did a great job. This is delicious. I haven't eaten in hours."

The furrow between her brows returned, stress etching itself into the edges of her face.

"Well, you're eating now, no worries."

She seemed to appreciate his response. It earned him a smile at any rate. He kept eating his stew.

"I wonder how long this investigation is going to last." Lily said.

"Could we just set all that aside for tonight? You need to relax, get some rest."

"I can't just forget it about it."

"Well, no."

"Can you?"

Forget the idea of her being in danger, being powerless to stop it, utterly in the dark as to who could be after her in the first place? Hardly.

His expression must have answered for him, because Lily's mouth curved up at one end into a tiny smile and then she said. "Exactly."

"So if you don't want to forget about it—"

"I didn't say that, I said I couldn't."

"Right, sorry. If you can't forget it about it, then what do you want to do tonight? Would you rather be left alone? I can show you the guest cabin after dinner. Or better yet, you can sleep in here, and I'll sleep in the cabin."

It wasn't that the guest cabin was less safe than his main house, it was just slightly more isolated. It sat behind the house, farther from the main road. Although that could be a good thing, too...

"I'm not kicking you out of your house, so it's the cabin, or I go back to mine."

Had he forgotten how much fire this woman had? Lily was not one to do anything easily.

"The cabin, then. I'll show it to you after dinner. Do you want to try to sleep, or we could try to talk through today, see if there are any avenues to investigate?"

Her eyes met his almost instantly. "Investigate?"

"Well, yeah."

"You said you weren't law enforcement anymore."

He felt the tension grow as she waited for an answer, and he waited to try to figure out exactly what he was going to say. "I'm not working as law enforcement right now," Travis confirmed. "But I'm still post certified."

"Which means?"

He shrugged. "I could go back to work if I wanted to."

"And why don't you?"

"Today sums it up pretty well. Would you want to run into stuff like that most days?"

He'd put it as gently as he could have, Lily felt, but the gist wasn't lost on her. No, she wouldn't want memories of people dying, covered in blood, haunting her dreams every night. It was hard enough that she'd had the few experiences she'd had with such things.

Well, really, just today's. Matt was the first person close to her who had died, but there had been no graphic violence, no terrifying scene to confront. Just uniformed men standing on her door and the absence of someone she cared deeply about.

There had been cracks in her and Matt's

relationship, of course, but every couple had their differences. Faith, for example. Lily had been raised to cling tightly to hers and Matt's approach to life had been less oriented toward such things. She'd found it somewhat insulting the way he patronized her a bit when they discussed faith, as though he was more intelligent for not believing... But besides that and some small squabbles, they'd had an ideal relationship. Smooth sailing.

Nothing like her and Travis. Fire and water if there ever was...

"Lily?"

She blinked, fighting to bring her mind back to the present conversation. "Yeah, I see why you wouldn't want to do that. Every day, I mean, or any day..." She shook her head. "It was awful."

"You should talk to someone about it. That's a lot to carry on your own."

"Who do you talk to?"

Travis hummed. "My oldest brother.

He's a counselor, so does that count more than just talking to a normal brother?"

Lily smiled. "Maybe it does. Maybe I should. For tonight, though, yeah, let's talk about it together. For the case, I mean, if that's okay."

Travis nodded. "Sure, for the case."

It was normal that she still felt a little drawn to him, wasn't it? That he was the first one she'd thought to call when she was in trouble? Surely that was to be expected, even with the years looming between now and when they'd been close. People didn't just forget a relationship.

The truth was, the way she felt for him was making her a little… Well, it wasn't making her nervous at all, and *that* made her nervous. He was taking care of her, keeping her safe. It was like no time had passed, yet Lily felt like she'd lived several lifetimes since then. How did that make any sense?

As she tried to untangle her thoughts,

it occurred to her that, honestly, she shouldn't try to quantify any of it. Travis was trying to keep her from being hurt or killed, and she appreciated that. Whatever she could tell him that might help him toward that goal, that was all tonight was about.

When they were finished eating, she helped him clear the dishes from the table and then washed them, much to his protest. Timber sat beside her on the kitchen floor, watching. She'd eaten her kibble when their dinner was cooking, though she did seem to be harboring some kind of hope that Lily might feed her scraps from dinner if only she looked cute enough.

Well, she wouldn't feed her too many, Lily thought as she tossed Timber a small bite of beef.

"Hot chocolate or coffee?" Travis asked from behind her, where he stood holding up two mugs.

"Hot chocolate would be great." Maybe it was a strange favorite drink for someone who ran a coffee shop, but there was nothing like hot chocolate, in Lily's opinion, to help you wind down after a stressful day. Or just enjoy the wrapping up of a good one.

It wasn't until he headed to the stove with a pot that she realized he meant to make his own.

"Wait, it doesn't always have to come from a packet?" she teased, and he laughed at her.

"You own a coffee shop, I'm pretty sure this comes as no surprise to you."

"Sure," she admitted, "but even I usually use chocolate powder with the sugar already added. This is next-level commitment."

"It's one of my favorite things. Still."

Oh, that was right. Her love for hot chocolate had developed in high school when she was dating Travis. Maybe it even developed because of him? Another bit of their past she'd forgotten or shoved to the back of her mind, maybe intentionally.

The silence as he made the hot chocolate wasn't companionable; it was awkward, and Lily knew it was her. Since they'd gotten to Travis's house, everything had been natural and cozy, almost too much so. Lily's emotions were too tumultuous to sort them fully, but if she felt so strongly connected to Travis still, was she being disloyal to Matt?

On the other hand, Matt was gone. Moving on would be expected. Healthy, even. But was it moving on if you were moving backward?

"You okay?" Travis handed her a mug of hot chocolate. "Careful," he warned as she took it, "it's hot."

"Thanks. Actually..." She trailed off, then cleared her throat. "I'm pretty tired. Maybe you could show me the cabin? I may need to call it a night pretty soon." She took a sip of the hot chocolate. It was so good she felt herself wishing she could sit down and savor it. But tonight was proof that she needed to be on her guard, not just for her physical safety but also for her emotions around Travis.

Not that he wasn't safe emotionally. He was. Too safe. That was the problem. Being around him made her feel like there was someone she could fully trust, someone she could open up to. Share her burdens. But she and Travis didn't have that kind of relationship anymore. Frankly, they didn't have *any* relationship anymore. He'd been the only one she could think to call. He apparently didn't want to see her hurt, and that was all.

On the trek across the lawn between his house and the cabin, Travis had to turn and wait for her a couple times.

"You're good, though?" he asked. "Besides being tired?"

Lily quickened her pace, aware of the dense woods on the edges of his property. It wouldn't take much for someone to hide there, lean against a tree, watch them... To what end, though? Lily didn't know of any reason she should be in danger.

But she also didn't know why anyone would have tried to burn down her house. Could someone truly be watching her now?

"I'm, uh..." She meant to say, yes, she was okay, then lock herself in the cabin and try to sleep. But try as she might, Lily didn't seem to be able to put on a face and pretend everything was okay today. It was like a full year of pretending to have everything together had finally caught up to her, and her expressions simply weren't willing to lie for her anymore.

"It's going to be okay." He started to reach for her hand, as if on impulse, then stilled, and he turned back to the cabin.

Of all the people she could have called for help. But who else was there? She and Matt had gotten so caught up in their whirlwind romance that her other friendships had sort of dropped away. She'd been busy. Distracted.

"This is it." Travis motioned to the cabin, and Lily took it in. The A-frame was classic, like something straight off social media. It was the type of place you'd go for a relaxing retreat. A bright red door was set into a wall of solid logs, adding a layer of warmth and playfulness. The attention to detail continued to surprise Lily as she eased the door open at Travis's invitation and stepped inside.

To her left was a small kitchen, an efficient style that she'd always pictured in tiny European cottages. There was a small table with two chairs beyond that, but most of the open space was a cozy living room, anchored by a fireplace on the back wall. Large windows on either side of the fireplace took full advantage of that view of the woods. There was a door off the living room.

"There are blinds." Travis motioned to the slim built-in blinds she hadn't noticed.

Lily felt herself relax a little. "Thanks, Travis. For letting me stay here and the hot chocolate and everything." Could she have chosen more inadequate words? He'd walked into a literal murder scene for her today, and all she could do was thank him for the hot chocolate and *everything*?

Still, when she forced herself to meet his eyes, she didn't see any kind of judgment. Instead his brown eyes were warm, like the cocoa they'd shared. He didn't touch her, didn't even reach for her hand, though somehow she felt her body warm as though he had.

"It really is going to be okay, Lily."

When he said it, she almost believed him.

FOUR

The sky wouldn't fully darken at all in late July, but Travis still found himself looking out the window, watching the shadows of the woods grow longer on the lawn, his eyes darting to the cabin entirely too often.

Was Lily really safe out there? He had second-guessed himself more than once since his return to his house. As safe as she was anywhere, he supposed. At least here she was close by. He'd have preferred she stay with him, but that hardly seemed appropriate to offer.

Stepping away from the window, he shoved a hand through his hair, then went through the motions of shutting the house down for the night. Dishes done. Counters clean. He turned off lights, then finally sat back down in a chair.

The silence should have been soothing, but it felt empty, heavy. It pressed against him, the blackness almost a tangible thing.

He sat with his eyes closed. Thinking.

If someone was specifically after Lily, there had to be a reason. Earlier, he'd satisfied himself that there was no way it was random. So why, then? It had been a long time since he'd investigated anything, and any good police officer knew that being emotionally invested in a case changed the angles they looked at. Being objective mattered.

Stepping back was an option, he supposed. He could just call the police department, follow up, make sure it stayed in the front of people's minds.

But realistically speaking, he knew how stretched thin law enforcement was in an area as geographically big as Alaska. He'd experienced it first-hand. When he knew he could help her, shouldn't he?

At the same time, how was he going to help? He didn't even know where to start.

He opened his eyes, now adjusted to the darkness, and sat, looking around and thinking. The man who'd been killed...who was he? Maybe he was the best place to start.

He pulled his phone out of his pocket to make a call, then realized how late it was. Tomorrow. He'd call tomorrow, get the guy's name, start there...

Even as he slid the phone back into his pocket, though, he realized he didn't need to call to get the name.

He knew it.

The man's height. Build. Last-seen location.

Which was the boat where Matt had

gone to arrest a ring of narcotics smugglers. That man had shoved Matt into the inlet.

The man who'd had the key and Lily's address in his pocket...was Arnold Harris, the one who had killed her fiancé.

Until Timber's whining woke her, Lily hadn't even been aware that she'd fallen asleep. She wasn't even in the bedroom of the small cabin, but in the living room—blinds closed, thank goodness— on the couch.

She'd fallen asleep with a notebook in hand, brainstorming everything she could about any reason someone might have for attacking her. So far the list was... nonexistent. She simply wasn't someone who gathered a lot of enemies. Last week someone had complained about having too much foam on a latte? But that hardly seemed worth killing over.

It made more sense that this was coincidental—maybe she'd found the body, and then someone had been scared she'd seen something up on the ridgeline and somehow figured out where she lived and set her house on fire to scare her. Except…then why had the dead man had her address in his pocket? That ruled out any flicker of hope in a coincidence.

That might have been about when she'd leaned back and closed her eyes, just to clear her head. She must have fallen asleep entirely.

Timber whined again, and Lily looked over at the dog. She was standing near the front door, eyes on one of the front windows.

Her phone. She needed her phone. Lily felt in her pockets and came up empty, fumbling around until she found it on the floor beside the couch. She must have dropped it when she fell asleep.

She texted Travis to let him know Timber was on alert and something might be wrong. She waited a couple seconds, her pounding heart threatening to beat out of her chest, then finally decided she was going to have to call.

Timber's hackles rose.

"Timber, come," Lily whispered in the most authoritative tone she could manage.

The dog obeyed immediately, and Lily was off the couch and moving toward the bedroom as quickly as she could. Or would it be better to go out the back door?

None of her options seemed particularly good. Barricading herself inside the cabin, even with Timber for protection, seemed naive. But running outside defenseless without a clue as to what she was facing didn't seem smart, either. The bedroom seemed like the best plan. She could go out the window in a pinch.

Her heartbeat quickened, and Lily fought for control over her emotions. She went to the bedroom window and tried to move the blinds aside just enough to see outside.

Beside her, Timber continued to growl, low and intimidating. Was it possible the dog was reading the situation wrong? Lily didn't think so, not with the way Timber had performed on the mountain. A police K-9 wouldn't simply forget all their skills just because they'd been injured. It was like having an extremely high-performing car when all she was really prepared for was a Honda Accord. Lily probably couldn't comprehend all that Timber was capable of. But it was clear that the smart, beautiful shepherd was not to be underestimated.

Because of that, maybe Lily could relax a little. Timber had this under control.

Once upon a time, she would have found comfort in believing that God had this under control. But that was ages ago. More than a year. Matt's death had changed things.

That wasn't true. She'd stopped asking God for things even before that, if Lily was honest with herself. Matt had always rolled his eyes at her faith, and then she'd started to think maybe it was childish of her to go to God with everything. She still believed in Him. It seemed incredible to her that some people didn't when evidence of Him was everywhere. Though she did think that He probably didn't want to be involved in her life quite as much as the church she used to attend had taught.

Travis had gone to that church, too. He'd believed that God was involved in all the details. Did he still feel that way? Or had he also changed as he got older?

Attention on the window, Lily was sure she was alone until three things happened at once.

Timber whirled around, hackles up—

she heard one footstep—and then there was the weight of a hand on her shoulder.

A scream built in her throat, and she opened her mouth to let it out when a hand clapped over it. Fighting with everything she had, it took at least three seconds to realize that the voice saying "it's me, it's me" belonged to Travis.

"What..." She scooted away from him, against the wall in the corner of the small bedroom. "What on *earth* are you trying to do? Kill me yourself?"

He rolled his eyes. "Obviously not. You texted, remember? So I came to help."

What she wanted to do was argue with the idea that every time she needed help, he came running, but hadn't it been true? For years, she'd told herself that Travis had broken her heart by asking her for something—marriage—that she hadn't been ready for, but the truth was he'd done everything for her. She just hadn't been able to give him the commitment he wanted.

Maybe she'd broken his heart?

"Okay, sorry. I'm sorry," she whispered. "But someone's out there, and I thought..."

"That I was whoever it is?"

"Exactly."

Timber had relaxed when she'd seen Travis, as though his presence took some of the weight of responsibility off her shoulders, but now she was eyeing the window again.

Then, just as quickly, she stopped. Turned to the bedroom door.

"I don't get it."

Travis shook his head. His jaw was tense, and she could practically see the storm clouds in his eyes.

"How did you get in?" she asked.

"Back door."

"No one around out there?"

"No."

Even though she'd been jolted awake, fatigue still pressed in on her. How she could be so tired with everything going on right now?

Timber stopped growling.

Frowning, Lily looked at Travis. "What's going on?"

But the way he shook his head, she could tell that he didn't know, either.

They waited like that for several more minutes, but nothing else happened. Had the danger really passed?

"Travis..." she started, but he interrupted her.

"Listen, there's something you have to know."

"Okay."

His tone was serious, and she found herself studying his face for some sign of what he was about to say.

It was strange how familiar his face still was, though time had matured it.

His jawline was more defined than it had been when they were in high school—it coordinated nicely with the broadening of his shoulders. His eyes had always betrayed his emotions, but to Lily, they were even stormier and more full of feeling now.

"The guy who you found dead?" he continued finally.

She waited.

"It was a guy named Arnold Harris, the man who's wanted for Matt's murder."

He hadn't meant to startle her with the information, but though the immediate danger seemed to have passed, he wanted her to be prepared for anything.

He wasn't sure what to think about that fact that the prime suspect in Matt's murder was dead. The man's death had been murder, for sure, it didn't matter what crimes he'd committed—Travis didn't condone any kind of vigilante justice. But who had killed him? Someone seeking revenge for Matt's death? Had his own gang killed him as punishment?

Travis would have guessed that execution-style killings were more the speed of this particular gang, though. They were one of the largest operations in Alaska, and it struck him that they'd have been less...passionate about the man's murder. Multiple stab wounds? That belied entirely more emotion than what a gang like that would do.

She spoke after a few moments. "How do you know?"

"I remember his face. So many wanted posters, I can't believe it took me this long to remember it."

"And you called someone currently at the police department to confirm?"

"Not yet, I figured in the middle of the night they had more on their minds. But I will."

Lily nodded, seeming to take it in. "What does this mean? What does it change?"

For her? Nothing. Her life was still in danger, and he had no clear ideas as to why.

But it might change things for the police department. "Chances are good it'll be bumped up in priority," he began. "Not that you weren't important, but now it's part of an open investigation where resources are already directed, which might make things move faster."

Her face seemed to say that she understood. He watched her for a minute as she sat without saying anything. Then she moved to stand.

"Where are you going?" he asked.

"The danger has passed, right? So no need to stay sitting on the bedroom floor."

She was right. He just hadn't quite managed to think past telling her who the dead man was. He followed her out into the living room.

"So what do you think?" she asked. Her tone was a little hesitant, he thought, but that made sense given the circumstances.

"About?"

"Tonight. Do we go outside? Try to find whoever it was?" She sounded about as doubtful about that as he felt. It didn't seem like a good plan in the middle of the night.

If he was on this case in an official capacity, yes, he'd go outside, try to find evidence of whoever had been lurking and see if they'd left anything behind that could be used as evidence, forensic or otherwise. Cases were often solved by the smallest details.

But if he were investigating this officially, he wouldn't have Lily with him. The chances of her staying put inside while he went out were slim, he assumed. He could tell her to stay, and maybe she'd listen, but Lily had never been big on taking orders.

"Will you stay inside?" he asked. He really had no business ordering her around anyway.

She looked at him for a second or two, then nodded. "Yeah, I'll stay. How long will you be gone?"

Already moving toward the front door lest she change her mind or he lose his nerve—it had been awhile since he'd done this—he answered, "Not long. If you haven't heard from me in half an hour, probably better call someone."

"Like the police?"

"Yep, that would be good. Lock the door behind me." He looked at Timber. "Stay." While he'd have sworn the shepherd rolled her eyes, she at by Lily's side as he reached to shut the door.

"Wait."

Lily's voice was enough to stop him in his tracks.

"Take her with you. You know you need her. She'll find things faster."

She wasn't wrong.

"Timber, come."

And just like that, the dog was at his side, as she'd been so many times in the past. She'd been Matt's K-9 partner, technically speaking. But Travis and Matt had worked together so much that Travis had worked with Timber almost as much as his friend had.

Shutting the door behind him and waiting until he heard the reassuring click of the lock, he gave Timber the command to search. Off leash, she searched for the trail that anyone nearby would have inevitably left. Very little of the scent would have dissipated in such a short time, so Timber should be able to tell him exactly where they had been hiding out—and whether they'd been preparing to come inside.

What had their goal been? No shots had been fired. There actually didn't appear to be anything amiss, at least to his eyes.

Timber ran from the front door and swerved to the right, toward the woods that sheltered the side of the house.

Travis always found so much peace in those woods but now he saw them as a liability, making it more difficult to see if someone was back there hiding. Waiting. He didn't hear anything, and looking at Timber, he didn't think she did, either. But she sure smelled something.

The dog continued determinedly into the woods. Then her pace slowed. Had she lost the scent? Or was she simply being cautious?

He called her to his side, petted her shoulder. Stopped. Looked. Listened.

People called it gut instinct, intuition

and any number of other things—Travis suddenly felt like he wasn't alone. It wasn't anything he could pinpoint exactly, not like he'd heard a noise or anything. No movement caught his eye. Absolutely nothing seemed out of place in the dark woods.

Timber's body language had relaxed beside him. Travis thought about the way they moved in the woods, weaving here and there, almost in a circle, away...

Away from the house.

Chills chased down his arms. "Timber, come."

He didn't care about being heard now, didn't care if someone started shooting at him. Let them, at least then he'd know they weren't shooting at Lily. Right now, he had no such reassurance.

Travis had messed up. Big time. Leaving her alone and taking the dog...

It had made sense on paper—Timber

was the most reliable way to search for evidence—but it had also been the most predictable course of action. And whoever was after Lily had predicted it. Law enforcement? Search and rescue? Someone who was just good at putting himself in other people's shoes?

He almost muttered a word he hadn't said in a good five years as he ran through the woods back toward the cabin, calves burning. He was sprinting in boots, not really his first choice, but he had been in a hurry when he'd left the house, focusing on getting to Lily as quickly as possible, and not considering a possible foot chase.

That was two mistakes tonight, both possibly big ones. If he was going to do this, he needed to help Lily, not get her hurt due to his negligence. He used the anger to push himself faster and was entering the clearing for the cabin before he knew it.

Everything looked the same. His human eyes simply couldn't gauge how concerned he should be. Instead, he looked down at Timber. She had easily kept pace with him and had the audacity not to be the slightest bit winded. She was alert, ears slightly forward, nose up.

Hackles raised.

He had not imagined this danger, had not jumped to the wrong conclusions.

"Easy," he told her as they moved toward the cabin. The front door was still shut, but Timber headed instead toward the back of the house. Travis followed.

Suddenly, the dog sprinted ahead, like a spring that had been released. She dashed around the house and straight through the back door that had very much not been open when they'd left.

Travis's chest squeezed with the most fear he'd ever felt—even more than yesterday. Now he knew how deeply they were entangled in a criminal case that had already cost the police department one of its best. He ran inside.

He heard Lily scream before he could see anything, and the sound terrified him. Vision adjusting, he saw Timber stopped in the doorway to the bedroom, looking like she was assessing her next move. Beyond her, he could barely see figures—Lily and someone else, someone larger.

Travis shouted the command for attack.

Timber leaped into the room, and he heard a man gasp in pain at the bite she delivered. If he'd still been law enforcement, he'd have had to warn the man that it was coming, but because he wasn't, the dog could bite without warning.

He dashed into the bedroom and saw Lily on a blood-smeared floor, and he could see blood, but couldn't tell how much or from where. He could hear her shuddered breaths, though, like she was holding back tears or trying to manage pain, so he knew without a shadow of a doubt that she was alive. Injured...but alive.

FIVE

Lily wasn't even sure where the pain was coming from, only that it was intense. Her arms felt bruised from the struggle, and the man had had something...a knife? She couldn't think about it yet—not when her dog and Travis were both in danger. Because of her.

That thought stung nearly as much as the bruises on her upper arms.

Fighting against the pain and the fear sliding around inside her, she crawled toward where Timber and Travis were both fighting with the attacker. She called Timber off and in the split second after the dog moved, Travis delivered a kick to the man that seemed to hit its mark.

"You all right?" Travis asked quickly, scanning her.

Out of the corner of her eye, she saw the man with the mask stumble to his feet and pull his arm back.

"Travis, watch out!"

Her warning came soon enough that Travis wasn't knocked down by a full hit. Instead, the punch glanced off his nose, and Travis closed his eyes instinctively with a yell.

Before the attacker could press his advantage, Lily told Timber to attack. This time, the man seemed to have had enough—he ran for the door, but not before he kicked out behind him, connecting with Timber hard enough for the dog to yelp.

"Timber!" Lily tried to crawl toward her, but the pain in her side made her double over. What was that? A rib? Something else?

Timber was already up and sprinting after the masked man. Was he seriously going to get away again?

The pain in Lily's side told her, yes, he was. She certainly couldn't chase after him, and Travis appeared to be regaining his bearings after taking a punch to the face.

"Timber!" she yelled again, but the dog ignored her, as if driven by a desire stronger than the one she usually had to please Lily.

"Lily, stop," Travis said, dropping to her side and breathing hard. "Don't go after him, it's not worth it."

She knew he was right. All she wanted was to find her attacker and kick him in his own ribs, which probably wasn't the right way to handle things, but he'd threatened her life more than once. She wanted him gone, put away in jail. She didn't want to know that he was out there, waiting. Next time, he'd probably do worse.

She had a feeling this had all just been a warning so far. Surely if he'd been trying to kill her, he would have?

It hurt her mind to even think this way. Why would a human want to harm another? She couldn't fathom what could be of this much importance. If she somehow had something they wanted, she would gladly give it back. Nothing was worth this.

This was why the world needed men like Matt, like Travis, who were willing to take risks and make sure people like that were behind bars instead of terrorizing others.

Why on earth had Travis quit? Not the time to ask, she knew, but she did want to know. One day, maybe it was a subject she could broach with him.

"Are you all right?" she asked him.

"What can I do?" She felt a little silly, because clearly she wasn't in much of a position to help.

On the floor beside her, Travis rubbed his face and looked over at her. "Me? What about you?"

"I'm…" She trailed off. Ultimately she couldn't lie to him. She was not fine, and she was not in any position to pretend otherwise, not when moving made her wince.

"You're in worse shape than I am, I think," he told her. "I shouldn't have taken my eyes off him."

"You were checking on me. It wasn't like you just weren't paying attention."

"Mistake number three," he muttered.

Lily didn't ask but noted his frustrated tone.

Timber ran back into the room, panting, but otherwise okay. Lily checked her over carefully, noting the tightness of her muscles but not seeing any broken skin or signs of blood. Nowhere that seemed overly tender. She felt some of her own tension leave her shoulders.

As soon as Timber had come back, Travis had gone out into the cabin's living area. He came back into the bedroom now, face looking slightly less tense. "Doors are locked. He's gone. And based on Timber's behavior, I think for real this time. Want to sit in the living room? I called 911, they're sending an ambulance."

She frowned at him. "I'm not going anywhere."

"Fine, but they're at least checking you out."

"Just right here, no hospital?"

It wasn't as though he could force her to go; she was an adult. So he nodded. "Just let them see how you are."

They sat in silence until the EMTs got there.

"Looks like there's some serious bruising developing." The EMT gently palpated her ribs, and Lily gasped as pain radiated through her midsection.

"It hurts." The understatement wasn't lost on her.

"You've definitely done some damage but I don't think anything's broken. Just bruised." As the EMT stood, he looked down at her and frowned a bit. "Even so, I'd really feel better if you came in."

"I'm fine."

Much as it was clear this wasn't his preference, he didn't argue with her, instead giving her a regimen of drugs and rest that was good enough for Lily.

Travis walked him to the door, locked it and returned to where she sat on the couch.

She watched as Timber followed him back to her. "How did whoever is after me get past her last time?"

Travis's face looked serious, and he glanced down at Timber. "Hard to say.

She was tracking a scent, but the woods are thick with scent, and sometimes it's difficult to differentiate…"

Was it her imagination or had his voice trailed off? She waited.

"And I don't know," he finally went on, settling into a chair opposite her. "I guess maybe she seemed a little off? She's trained, very well trained, but this isn't what she's trained for. This is more personal protection, with some searching thrown in. She knows the commands, she knows the skills, but contextually that could be affecting how she behaves, at least a little."

Only some of what he said made sense to Lily, but she thought she understood what he was trying to say. Timber was extremely smart and knew what to do, but the weirdness of this situation, her being retired and then suddenly being asked to work by both of them… It wasn't quite what Lily had expected out of life, either.

Maybe people weren't the only ones who had to adjust their expectations. The thought almost made her smile. It definitely made her feel a little less alone and even more connected to her dog than she'd felt before.

She reached over and petted Timber, then sighed, closed her eyes and leaned back against the couch. How had life turned so complicated? Yesterday morning, she'd been a woman trying to heal. She'd been grieving, yes, but working on healing. She enjoyed running her coffee shop, coming up with new scones to sell, exploring outside. Overall, she was pretty happy.

Immediately her conscience gave her a gentle nudge. Happy? That was overstating it. Lily felt…not unhappy. A little empty. Sometimes frantic to find something to fill the space in her heart and mind. Lonely.

And as much as she did miss Matt, at least the happier times they'd had— things had been stressful there at the end, but she didn't like to dwell on that now, it didn't feel fair—she missed even more how her life had been simple and uncomplicated.

Maybe the emptiness was just part of getting older.

Or maybe Lily missed the innocent faith she'd had as a child, the way she would talk to God like He really heard her.

She swallowed hard, then looked over at Travis. He seemed to be studying her. Did he know, could he tell that she'd mostly walked away from what they'd both believed, at least functionally speaking?

Lily somehow hoped he didn't. The idea of disappointing him didn't sit well with her, and she knew he would be disappointed.

"What are you thinking?" he asked.

She froze. Then decided they'd gone long enough without talking.

Maybe it was the lateness of the hour and her defenses were down, but suddenly being honest with him felt like the right thing to do.

"About faith…" She trailed off, and Travis felt like she was choosing her words with more care than she would have at one point. Delicately. That was how she treated them now.

"Yeah?" He made himself relax his shoulders a little, even as his insides tensed.

"I just don't know anymore, Travis. I mean, do you? You've seen stuff now as a police officer that surely you couldn't have fathomed before."

"So what are you saying?" What did she not know?

"Matt believed in God and all of that, but Matt also thought that He's not so involved as we like to think He is, you know?"

If she was looking for agreement, she wouldn't get it from him. Travis was far from perfect, but if there was one thing he was sure of, it was that God was even more present in their daily lives than they realized, not the opposite. "So Matt's beliefs influenced yours?"

"I think he just helped me see what I hadn't wanted to." She stopped, as if waiting for him to speak, but when he didn't answer, she continued, "That God is real but I need to stop bothering Him."

"You're not bothering Him."

"He's busy, Travis. Keeping the world going and all of that?" She shook her head. "Anyway. I was just thinking about what I used to believe."

"I can see why the topic would be on your mind." Now it was his turn to pick his words with intention. The last thing he wanted to do was push Lily away, but this was so far from what they'd been raised to believe, from what she'd used to cling so tightly to.

She shrugged, and he thought she looked a little more tired than she had earlier. And it didn't seem like just a middle-of-the-night sort of tired. Maybe her exhaustion wasn't just from the stress, but from the weight of trying to carry everything all alone?

He found himself praying without even thinking about it. *Help her, God. Be with her, bring her back.* If she wasn't going to talk to God for herself right now, Travis could at least bring her to God in prayer. It wouldn't be the same as having her own relationship, but it was what he could do right now.

"Yeah. That, the past... All of it. I

never meant to disappoint you, Travis. With this, or…you know, before."

They were going there? Right now in the wee hours of the morning on this couch, still unsure who was after her and why?

"You could never disappoint me." His words were firm.

"That's not true."

"Of course it is."

"I disappointed you before, you know I did."

No. She'd hurt him and made him wish… Well, he wasn't sure what he wished. Was there something he could have done differently?

Not really, but he did wish maybe that their love had been enough, ridiculous as that sounded. He wished he'd been enough for Lily, but she'd had dreams she wanted to chase, and her fear of never realizing those dreams had overshadowed what they had.

"You didn't. Maybe just broke my heart a little." He said it with a smile, figuring if she was going to be honest, he owed it to her to be honest, too. Besides, it was better than her thinking she'd disappointed him.

"I'm sorry about that," she said.

"I know."

She didn't say anything else, and Travis was content to sit there in silence. He watched from his chair as Lily leaned her head back against the couch and closed her eyes. One hand was on Timber's head, which was resting neatly on her paws where the dog was curled up on the couch.

Moments later, Lily jerked, like she'd fallen asleep and woken up.

"I'm not going anywhere," he told her quietly. "Just go to sleep."

To his surprise, that was exactly what she did. It didn't take more than a minute or two for her to nod off again. This time, she didn't fight it.

His heart ached as he watched her, both for how much physical pain she must be in and also for her spiritual state. For her to have stopped believing that God really cared was heartbreaking to him. How hard it must be for her to live that way. He tried to imagine what it would be like, but it was too much to consider. He wasn't any kind of perfect person, not the kind of guy people would label as *saintly* by any stretch of the imagination, but he was very aware of his need for God. Travis talked to Him throughout the day. Living that way was almost second nature at this point.

Once upon a time, Lily had had that, too. While Travis was aware there was some kind of agreed-upon code never to think badly of someone who had died, he did have to resist the urge to think of all the ways Matt had failed her.

Yeah, his friend hadn't been able to control getting killed in the line of duty, and he'd been a hero. But Matt hadn't been there for Lily emotionally before he'd died, at least not to the degree that Travis felt like someone should support. He'd tried hard not to pay attention to their relationship—it made working conditions too weird between him and Matt—but he'd heard the tail end of enough phone calls in the months before Matt's death to know there had been trouble in paradise.

He also found himself angry at the way Matt had effectively led her away from her faith, at least to some degree. It was useless getting upset with a dead man, though, and a complete waste of energy. Instead he tried to turn his attention to praying for her, asking God to help them get through this and quickly find out who was after her. He begged God to keep her safe.

Then he looked over at her while she slept, noting the way her hair fell softly across her forehead, the way her lips parted just a little when she fully relaxed. And he debated whether or not he was brave enough to pray for a second chance with her. Was that something he was even prepared for? It would be a risk for him, too, as he'd not walked away unscathed the last time…

Her coming back into his life was the most dangerous thing for him. Not only would he walk in front of anyone threatening to harm her, but he was fully ready to try again with their relationship, if he was honest with himself. He felt like he should have hesitations—he certainly saw the logical ones that were there—but in his heart, he had none.

Just give me wisdom, please, God, he prayed. *Help me to know if this is something I need to pursue, maybe when things are safe for her again, and she's not a target anymore.*

He found himself looking around the room, imagining the last few hours and the terror Lily must have felt when she realized she was alone with a killer.

Help me to be wise. I have a feeling I'm going to need that. Whoever this is has the advantage in almost every way, but God, You're on our side. Help us figure this out. Help her to stay safe.

Another glance at Lily.

And God, help me to win her heart again if that's what You want.

Travis stood and did a circuit of the cabin, listening for anything out of the ordinary. Satisfied all was well, he went back to the living room, watched Lily sleep and smiled.

He was going to help her. He was going to make up for all the ways he'd failed her before. And maybe…

Maybe then he was going to try again.

SIX

She'd never felt quite so relieved to walk through the back door of her little coffee shop, partially because she'd missed it, and partially because she'd had the uncomfortable feeling in the parking lot that she was being watched. She felt herself relax as she locked the door behind her. The shop smelled like rising cinnamon rolls that Hannah, her baker, had come in to make earlier, and like coffee beans. Always the smell of coffee beans. Initially she'd planned to roast her own coffee beans on-site, but when she'd discovered that the smell of freshly roasted coffee and the smell of roasting coffee were quite different, and that there were plenty of local roasters who made better roasts than she did, she decided to stock local things and focus on her favorite aspects of the business.

One of those favorites was the ambiance itself, the idea of creating a space for community where people could be comfortable. She'd spent long hours choosing details about the flooring, the light fixtures—industrial-style Edison lights, some with wire cages for dramatic emphasis, hanging over individual tables, and strands of Edison lights all across the top of several other walls. The warmth of the room was undeniable, even before she'd lit the fireplace.

She lit it now, and while she'd intended to go right to work, she found herself sliding into one of the booths.

All of this had been…a lot, to put it mildly. She'd come to work today thinking it might be good to keep something in her life consistent, and she was sure now that it had been the right choice. So much had changed since she impulsively called Travis.

How could someone go from being such a huge part of her life to not being in it at all, then back in it again? Maybe she needed to spend less time thinking about this, but try as she might, Lily was finding Travis a huge distraction.

Reliving the past had its consequences. She had slept well enough last night, but she'd dreamed entirely more than she would have preferred. Mostly about Matt, some about Travis and some about being alone in a dark room. All of the dreams had tangled into a nonsensical swirl. She vaguely remembered tossing and turning.

Resting her elbows on the smooth wooden surface of the booth's table, she took a deep breath.

The bell over the door chimed, and she looked up to see Hannah, the baker.

"Morning, boss." Hannah smiled in her direction.

"Very funny." Though it was true that Lily was Hannah's employer, the two of them had been friends for years.

"Everything okay? The message you left was kind of vague."

Lily had left Hannah a hurried voicemail early in the morning, attempting to explain why she might be late today, but Lily was sure it hadn't made much sense. She hadn't wanted to worry her unnecessarily.

"Yeah, I think so. Mostly." The less Hannah knew, the better. The last thing Lily wanted was to put her friends in danger.

"Sitting with your head in your hands like that doesn't really give that impression, just so you know."

A solid point. Lily attempted a smile. "It's…it's a lot of things."

Hannah was kind enough not to press

her, and the two of them fell into their usual morning routine of getting ready for the day. Her customers started coming through right on time, and Lily let herself be distracted for a few blissful hours. Even though she knew she could only ignore her own life for so long.

Timber seemed as though she was staying on alert. Usually she slept soundly on the floor of the coffee shop at the end of the front counter, but today one ear was always perked as though she was merely napping and ready to snap into action if the occasion warranted it.

It was just before four, almost time to close, when the door chimed. Hannah let out a low whistle. Lily turned.

It was Travis, dressed casually in jeans and a long-sleeved plaid shirt. He looked exactly like what she would expect to see if she Googled handsome man who works at hardware store.

Should Lily feel butterflies in her stomach at his presence? Nothing the least bit romantic had happened between them recently. But he'd been so easy to talk to and hadn't judged her for the way her faith had changed. Travis always had been a keeper. Maybe she'd been foolish not to keep him.

On the other hand, how could she question her past choices when those choices had led to her standing in the coffee shop she owned and seeing her dream come to life? She'd chased her dreams *without* destroying anyone else's life. If only her own mother had realized how badly she wanted to pursue her dreams before she'd made other choices.

Then again, Lily might not be here if she had.

"Travis, hi," she finally said, shifting her attention to the person currently in front of her and away from her mother, who might as well be a figment of Lily's imagination. "How was your day?"

"Good. Yours?"

She heard the uncertainty in his voice and smiled, hopefully in a way he would find reassuring. "It's been fine. Boring, even."

"Nothing suspicious?"

"Not in the slightest." And it was true. People had been their normal selves, she'd sold various coffee drinks, Hannah had baked and helped run the front. Timber had not once alerted. It was like it had all been a dream. Not entirely a bad one—Lily was finding it was nice to be on speaking terms with Travis again—but a dream she was ready to see the end of anyway.

"Did you learn anything?" she asked, and he hesitated, his eyes flickering toward where Hannah was cleaning up behind them.

Finally he nodded. "Later. My house for dinner?"

"Yeah, I guess we'd better. I still haven't

heard from the fire department about mine."

"I'll stay while you close up if that works for you."

She didn't mind terribly, though she was hoping it hadn't come to that. Then she thought back to that morning and how she'd had a slight sensation of being watched as she walked into the coffee shop.

"You didn't follow me to work and watch me this morning, did you?" she asked.

Travis shook his head.

A shiver ran down her spine. So either she'd imagined it entirely, or it had been someone other than Travis. Neither option was reassuring.

Telling Hannah good-night once the shop was properly closed, Lily locked the door behind her and started walking to her car. Travis walked with her, looking both ways intently. Lily thought that if she was going to keep this on the down-low at all, he was going to have to look a little less like a bodyguard and a little more like a friend who just happened to stop by.

Then again, it was a small town. People were going to talk either way. But after the news articles that ran after Matt's death and having people talk about "poor Lily" all last year… Lily just wanted to fly under the radar for a bit. For once, she'd like not to be the woman with the story that demanded pity.

Once they arrived at Travis's house, he wasted no time telling her what he'd learned, which was very much like him.

"The man was definitely the one we believed was responsible for Matt's death," he began.

"Wow." Lily shook her head. "I know you told me that was likely but knowing for sure…" She'd felt so bad about not being able to help him. Did she still feel that way, knowing he'd killed Matt? She'd like to think she wasn't the kind of person who believed in vigilante justice. Still, it was eerie. Especially when she considered that the day the man had died was the one-year anniversary of Matt's death...

It was too coincidental.

"It's weird," Travis said slowly, almost like he could read her thoughts.

"It is, yes. What do you think? Any idea who could be behind this?"

"With what we know?" He inhaled deeply. "I really think it's someone from the narcotics group that Matt was investigating when he was killed."

It wasn't something Matt had talked much about. But Lily had known in the days before he died that he'd been fairly deep undercover, working with a narcotics group in the hope of bringing them to justice. She was aware of how drugs had left their mark on the Last Frontier, leaving so many Alaskans homeless and hopeless, destroying lives, families and more. The work he was doing had seemed worthwhile, though it had taken a toll. At the end, he'd been even more short-tempered than usual. He'd told her he was fine, but the dark circles under his eyes had said he wasn't sleeping well. Lily hadn't known how to help him, and she'd felt them drifting apart.

Then he was gone, and it was like her future had been stolen from her the night his was stolen from him.

Honestly, she was only just starting to feel like maybe she could move on. She didn't know about falling in love again, but in most ways she could move on. And now…what? She was going to just step right back into the nightmares of her past?

Deciding she should get clarification before she went into full panic mode, she asked, "And I'm guessing the only way to figure out who is behind this is to look back at Matt's case, see who was involved and do a little investigating of our own?"

Much as she tried to keep the anxiety from her voice, Travis still knew her better than that, and she could feel his concern as he studied her. Attempting to look unfazed, Lily stayed silent under his scrutiny.

"I think that's what will help lead us to our suspect the fastest, yes," Travis said, not doubting his own words for a second. "But I'm not sure that's what's best for you."

What did Lily even know about that case? He doubted she'd seen anything like the case records, as there would be no reason to let those leave the police department. He could probably get his hands on a copy of them, or at least a chance to look at them, with his connection to APD and his post certification. But Lily had probably just been told Matt was killed in the line of duty and then left with only questions.

"What's best for me is for this to be over." She was shaking her head, her eyes closed. "Or better yet, for none of it to have happened in the first place."

"The second would be my vote, but we don't have that option."

Her face said that she knew he was right, and Travis wasn't surprised. Lily had never been much for playing the victim. She'd rise to the occasion, he knew she would.

But how far would she go to solve it? He still had concerns that it would be too far. And Lily couldn't possibly know what that was, she'd never poured her heart and soul into solving a case and then watched it slowly take over. She hadn't spent hours contemplating the worst of what humanity was capable of.

"I need to be able to move on with my life," she said. "And I can't do that if I'm looking over my shoulder all the time. Someone wants..." She shrugged. "Wants something from me. To hurt me? Scare me?"

"Someone wants to kill you, most likely."

"Doesn't that seem like an overreaction? I mean, I didn't see anything except the body. Okay, we found a key and an address on him, but the address was to my house. It's not like I stumbled upon some new place."

She had a point, but it still made no sense. She was clearly in danger, but what did the person after her have to gain by scaring her? This was the part of police work he'd hated the most, the need to climb into the mind of a criminal and guess what they were thinking.

As a sane individual who liked to stay on the right side of the law, Travis didn't want to be able to imagine what they were thinking, not really.

"I understand you want to be able to move on with your life," he began, shifting on his living room sofa, "but this is going to be tough."

Her eyes flashed when she turned to him. "I think I can handle something tough."

A couple seconds of silence. "Look," he said at last, "I didn't mean it like that. Of course you can handle it."

She was already shaking her head. "No, I appreciate that you don't want me to have to handle things like this. That's what you meant, right? Not that I can't?"

No matter how many years had passed, she clearly still understood him. Once upon a time, they had barely needed words to communicate, they'd been that in sync with each other.

"That's what I meant, yes." Then he admitted defeat. "If you really want to do this, let's get in my car. I'll drive us to the police department and get the records, and see what we can work through."

She smiled. He gathered his keys and headed toward his car with Lily and Timber following to join him. They drove toward Anchorage, swinging through a coffee stand on their way.

He ordered his typical triple shot Americano and started to order Lily's latte with sugar and whip when he realized he didn't know her anymore.

When he paused, she smiled. "Same coffee. Same as it always was."

That was the problem, wasn't it? Some things did seem like they were the same, but Travis knew in his heart they were both different people. Right?

"Just like we used to do," Lily said when he handed over her coffee.

"Yeah, just like." Was it? How different were they now than they had been back then?

"I'm sorry…" she began.

"Listen, I appreciate that we aren't trying to dance around the past, but we were both young. No need to rehash everything, right?"

"Sure, right." She stumbled over the words.

Fearing that more conversation would take them down a road he just wasn't braced for, he kept driving.

Silvertip Creek was only about twenty minutes north of Anchorage, a bedroom community much like Eagle River or Chugiak, but the twenty minutes seemed to drag as they'd exhausted all safe topics. He kept his hands on the wheel, his eyes on the road. He wanted to pretend like the years that had passed meant something, but his heart had been in his throat when he thought she might be killed yesterday, when he'd realized that the intruder had intentionally led Timber on a wild goose chase through the woods…

Wait. Intentionally.

"What?" she asked.

"The man intentionally led Timber on a wild goose chase and covered the scent trails so he could double back to the house."

"Right, you said something…"

"Intentionally," he emphasized. "Otherwise it's almost too coincidental. Which means this is someone who knows how search dogs work, or police dogs."

"Dramatically narrowing our field of suspects."

But something still nagged at him. He frowned, an uneasy swirl developing in his gut. "So someone who works with dogs…"

"Why don't you seem happy? Doesn't this make it easier?"

Easier and harder at the same time, Travis thought. "The thing is," he said slowly, "we already narrowed it down to someone likely within the narcotics gang."

Lily's eyes met his, and he saw in their clear blue the same understanding he'd just come to. "No," she said quietly. "Someone involved in the case?"

"Someone investigating it, probably. Or at least close to the investigation." Travis shrugged. "I can't guarantee it one way or another, obviously."

"Sure." Her voice betrayed her discomfort with the idea. Who liked the idea of a dirty cop? Or a search-and-rescue worker who went bad? No one. Travis had turned off more than one movie because of a similar plot line.

"Whoever it is, Lily, we're going to figure it out. I promise." He meant it.

He'd started off intending to keep her safe, but she needed more than that. She needed to know this threat was gone and that she could go back to living her life.

And Travis was determined to give her what she needed.

SEVEN

What struck Lily most about the trip to the Anchorage Police Department was how glad everyone was to see Travis. When he told her he'd changed jobs, she knew it hadn't been for any kind of job failure. Travis was too good a man and too good at what he did for that to be a concern. But she had wondered if there was any kind of weirdness at work that made him not want to be there. It wasn't something she could picture any more, though; from the time they walked into the glass-and-metal building, the whole department treated him like a long-lost hero.

"Travis Beckett!" An older man beamed

at him from behind the front desk. "You're back!"

"Only for a couple of questions."

A shadow cross the man's face. "Narcotics case?"

Travis nodded. "And yesterday's victim."

"I figured. Officer Knox is working it. I'll show you back."

For the first time, the man seemed to notice Lily. He opened his mouth and stuck out his hand as if to introduce himself, then paused as if he recognized her. Lily didn't know how. It wasn't like she'd come to the police office; Matt had kept his personal life and work life very separate.

Besides the fact that he was coincidentally engaged to his police partner's ex-girlfriend. Besides that.

The man showed them down a hallway that looked like it belonged in any kind of office building. But Lily knew

behind some of those doors were inter-
rogation rooms, behind others shelves
and shelves of evidence.

Police work was fascinating to her,
probably because it had been Travis's
plan since high school and he'd spent
so much time talking about it. Had that
been part of what attracted her to Matt?
Maybe. She hadn't known he was Travis's partner, though, or she'd never have
agreed to go out with him at all. By the
time she found out, she was already involved with Matt.

"Here you go." The older man paused
at a door. "It's good to see you, Beckett.
Don't be a stranger." He patted Travis
on the back and was gone.

Lily barely had time to process the in-
teraction when the door, opened almost
immediately to Travis's knock.

"Hey!" an officer exclaimed happily.
"About time! Back to get a job?"

"Definitely not."

"You can't seriously be enjoying small-town life?" He laughed. "Or maybe you are?" His eyes moved to Lily. "Who is this?"

It was clear the man thought there was something between them. Not sure how to proceed, Lily waited for Travis to handle it.

"Knox, this is…" Travis trailed off, and who could blame him? How to encompass what they were to each other in a sentence or two? "My friend Lily."

She found her shoulders lowering with relief. If he had only defined her as Matt's fiancée… Well, she didn't want that. She wanted Travis to think of her just as her. Or maybe in the context of a woman he cared about. Which was terrifying. Should she be getting close to him again? What if he hurt her?

Or worse, what if she hurt him again?

Dragging her attention away from the

past, she tried to focus on the police officer standing with them.

It wasn't the first time she'd heard the man's name. Matt had spent plenty of evenings frowning, muttering about Officer Knox. He'd seemed extraordinarily stressed when his name or any others from the case—names she'd forgotten now—had come up. The longer he worked the narcotics case, the more his behavior had changed. He hadn't spent as much time with her, and when they were together, it was like she wasn't actually there. Or maybe it was like he wasn't there?

Matt had seemed like another person on that case, she realized. Would the same thing happen to Travis? For the first time, she took his warning from earlier seriously, that it was going to be tough if she wanted to dive into this more deeply. But what other choice did she have? She couldn't live like this.

Attempting to ignore the knowing feeling in her stomach, she listened to the men talk.

"You sure you want to wade back in?" the officer was asking Travis.

"I'm sure I have to." Travis motioned toward Lily. "She found the victim yesterday. Her and Timber."

It seemed she wasn't the only one with hesitations. Lily wasn't sure that made her feel any better. If anything, it made her feel worse.

Timber had waited in the car with the window down. As much as Lily hadn't wanted to leave her, she understood Travis's point that it might be strange for Timber to walk back into the building when she didn't have a job there anymore. Lily hadn't wanted to put her through that confusion.

"I can give you what we have on it, most of it." The officer was already sitting back down at a desk, pulling things up on a computer.

Lily always forgot that police records were digitized now, she liked to picture them in a dim basement room somewhere, lining the gray walls and containing all sorts of intrigue. They lost something on the computer, at least as far as atmosphere went, but hopefully the files would still reveal what they needed to know.

"Thanks," Travis responded.

She listened as the two men discussed some of the case's details. At one point, Travis alluded to Matt's death and Officer Knox cleared his throat and nodded as if to point out that Lily was there.

"She knows already," Travis admitted, finally disclosing what Lily wasn't sure she wanted him to. "This is Lily Peterson, Matt Davis's fiancée."

The other man didn't say anything that indicated a change; it was the way he held himself. Because she wasn't a random civilian, he seemed suddenly less guarded, with a slight bit of…what? Respect? Awe? Lily hadn't done anything heroic. She'd loved someone and then lost them in the line of duty. But she'd noticed several people treat her like this. Like she was different now.

And while she unquestionably was, she was getting awfully tired of being treated like it.

"I'm sorry for your loss," the officer said.

Lily had heard the words before more times than she could count. "Thanks. I appreciate your help now."

He nodded, then hit a button on his keyboard. "This should be good." A printer whirred and started spitting out sheets of paper. "Anything else you need, let me know."

As she watched the copied files stack up in the printer, with more words about this case than she'd have thought possible, Lily found herself hoping that maybe this was enough. They'd not solve the whole case, obviously, not when police had been working it fruitlessly for years. But if they could just find enough in those records to tell them who had killed the drug runner, get that person off her back and turned in to law enforcement where they belonged...then maybe she had a chance of having her life back.

It was funny. She'd fought so hard to have her own life that she'd even turned down Travis's proposal when she had loved him more deeply than she'd loved anyone, Matt included. But now she didn't fully know why she'd wanted that freedom so badly. She had her coffee shop, yes, a dream come true, but right now she couldn't even stay at her own house. She was the very definition of not free.

Hopefully something in these files would have the power to change that. Lily wanted another chance to live her life with something more like true freedom. And maybe make some different choices this time.

Her gaze darted to Travis. Did she believe in second chances?

She didn't know, but she wanted to get this case solved, get her life back and have a chance to find out.

Since Lily still hadn't heard from the fire department about when her house would be safe, they went back to Travis's. Lily offered to cook, but he told her he had it under control. Working with food all day at the coffee shop didn't seem likely to lend itself to her wanting to prep dinner after work. Besides, it was his kitchen, and he knew where everything was.

While Lily sat at the counter flipping

through the police department files, he prepped chicken Alfredo and salad. Mostly, though, he was watching her, seeing the emotions chase across her face as the details of the case were revealed to her.

"So he was undercover for a lot less time than I thought." Her mouth was scrunched a little into a frown.

"About six months, right?"

Lily nodded. "That's what this says."

As she flipped from page to page, Travis found himself imagining where she was in the whole saga.

"Why did you think he'd been undercover for more than six months?" he asked as he poured the noodles into the boiling water.

She answered without looking up. "I really thought he told me he was going undercover earlier than that? He definitely was harder to reach, more stressed, for longer than six months. I don't know, maybe I'm just remembering wrong."

Except Lily had always had an excellent memory. Her memorization skills were part of the reason she'd done so well in school, along with her natural intelligence. Travis had a hard time believing she'd mix up something like that. On the other hand, trauma did funny things to people, and losing Matt the way she had was bound to impact her mind, wasn't it?

She rubbed at her eyes. "There's so much here. This is ridiculous."

"It's a lot."

"We're never going to find whoever it is, are we? Not if they're buried in a case file thicker than the last book I read."

He figured that was a slight exaggeration, but due to the extensive nature of the narcotics ring Matt had been investigating, she was right that it was an extremely thick file. He walked over, flipped through some of it himself and laid the most important pages in their own stack.

"I'll comb through the rest of it when I have a chance," he promised.

"You have a full time job, too, though," she pointed out.

He appreciated that, though to him there was a difference between her dream job running her own business and him helping his brother out at his store. Police work had been his dream, but what if it had been the wrong dream? He just didn't see how he could keep doing that kind of work. And here he was, stepping into it again. Just a glance at the documents had confirmed his discomfort. Victim. Body. Quantities of drugs, lives destroyed and lost.

Why wouldn't it stop? Why couldn't he just walk away from it all?

Something within him knew that this would all go on whether he was in police work or not. At least in that capacity, he could battle against the darkness, not just ignore it. Not that he thought people who weren't in law enforcement were ignoring anything, not at all, but Travis knew deep in his heart that he had been hiding.

"I can handle it," he told her, hoping what he said was true in several ways.

Lily seemed to take him at his word. She shifted in her seat and started to focus on the smaller pile he'd left. As he set the table, she kept reading.

"So? What do you think?" he asked when the food was ready and on the table.

"I think I'm overwhelmed."

"Dinner, then?"

She nodded and moved to the table. He thought he saw the tension on her face ease when she saw the meal. "Wow," she said, "this looks amazing. Again. You really can cook."

Half wishing her affirmation didn't matter so much to him, he shrugged, but he was more thankful than she'd ever know that she thought his food was worthwhile. There wasn't much he could do for her. Sure, he could offer her a place to stay, but he couldn't actually offer her safety, which was what he really wanted to do. Food like this and maybe a few minutes to relax were the best he could do right now, and he liked that she seemed to appreciate it.

As he served them each food, she went on, "I still can't believe you did this. Do you cook like this when it's just you?"

He'd eaten sandwiches for the past two weeks straight. And not restaurant-quality sandwiches, either, but ham and cheddar with a little bit of mayo. He raised his eyebrows, and she laughed. Apparently she could tell what his answer was.

They ate in silence for a little while, and then Lily brought up the case files.

"So if I'm understanding correctly, this group is based in California, but has a…branch up here now?"

He had to hold back a laugh. He'd never really thought of drug-running operations in terms of branches—that sounded so businesslike—but Travis supposed there was some truth to the idea. This was a massive organization, albeit an illegal one. These weren't meth heads cooking drugs in a shed in the woods somewhere. These people were very intentional about the way their business ran, and yes, they'd expanded to Alaska.

"That sounds right," he admitted. "Anchorage PD had asked Matt to look into it…"

"Do you guys usually get asked? I mean, I always assumed you were just assigned things."

"They tend to ask when it comes to undercover assignments. If an undercover officer has too much going on personally, or just shouldn't be in that situation for whatever reason, it can turn bad really quickly."

"Is that what happened to Matt?"

"It shouldn't have been. I don't think so."

There was too much in how he'd died that was inconsistent with that idea. His cover hadn't been blown, really. It had only been that last day, when he'd gone to the boat to arrest Arnold Harris, that things had turned and Matt had been killed. Surely if the drug ring had any inkling that he was working for the police department, they'd have gotten rid of him before that. He'd been able to report all kinds of information to the department—the types of narcotics being smuggled, who might be involved, though he hadn't gotten any top names—it didn't make sense that they'd have willingly let him have all of that if they suspected he was really an under-cover officer.

Matt had put himself at risk and paid the ultimate price for it. Travis wished he'd been able to do more, but when Matt had been undercover, he'd been in charge of searching different locations with Timber, trying to stop the drugs as they came into Anchorage in vari-ous ways before they ended up leaving the city and infecting smaller towns and villages.

"Travis?"

Her voice had the tone of a person who'd been calling someone's name without being heard. He wasn't terribly surprised he'd gotten lost in his own head. It had been a rough case, and he was still working through it mentally. Judging by the emails he still got from friends at APD, and the references to the mandatory counseling some of them were still going through, he wasn't the only one who was having trouble moving on.

"What? I'm sorry, I was distracted."

Her face softened, like maybe she understood how hard this was to walk through again. He'd known it would be, he hated being reminded of all the ways people hurt each other, but he hadn't counted on being so overwhelmed by feelings of guilt. What if he could've done more, could have seen more, discovered more? Should Travis have been the one undercover? But he'd never been as good at it as Matt was. Matt had nerves of steel.

He wasn't sure that he was comfortable with the way she was studying him.

"Are you okay?" she asked, sounding more unguarded than before.

"Not really." What harm was there in answering her honestly? It wasn't like any kind of judgment she could have for him would impact their closeness now. She'd broken up with him once—surely by definition that meant they were not close. But at the same time, he knew that he was always honest with her about how he felt, and so was she.

Maybe that was a weird foundation, but it's what they had.

"I will be fine," he rephrased. "I think, one day."

"It couldn't have been easy standing back, not being the one to go under-cover."

"It wouldn't have been easy to go un-dercover, either. Nothing about that job is easy."

Lilly nodded as if pondering this. "So what did happen to Matt? I mean, I see the facts here."

He heard the unspoken words. The files were just facts, not explanations. Had she expected that these facts would answer questions she'd had, maybe give her some kind of closure? He didn't blame her, but he could have told her that wouldn't be effective.

"But you want to know what really happened," he filled in for her.

She nodded.

Travis took a deep breath and began.

EIGHT

"July 8 last year, we thought it was all going down. The meeting was set for midnight, when it would be mostly dark, and that seemed fitting for a case like this. Everyone was excited, I guess, because we had been chasing this narcotics ring for so many months, and from what Matt had told us, this was going to be the night. He had enough to take them down, but he hadn't reported much of it yet. He was so deeply embedded that he didn't feel like he could without getting caught."

That made sense to Lily. The last two weeks of Matt's life, she'd barely seen him. In fact, she'd been planning to have a conversation with him about their future and whether this was what she could expect, but she'd never gotten the chance.

"I was one of the ones who went with him. Me, Chief McDowell, Officer Knox. We were positioned at various points near the drop site, which was along Knik Arm, almost to the valley, near Chugiak. I was the closest to the boat."

As he spoke, she could hear his voice tightening as he thought of what was coming next in the story. Of course Lily knew also, but it didn't make it any easier to brace herself.

"The first sign that everything hadn't gone according to plan was that there was only one person on the boat that came to meet Matt. He'd taken a small craft to the beach and was waiting, and from the way he'd talked, half of the gang was supposed to be on this boat. But it was just one guy."

"The man from the other night," she filled in, and he nodded.

"Yeah." He took a deep breath. "They started to argue. We didn't want to ruin Matt's cover, so we'd been told to wait until we were sure it was time to make the arrests. I couldn't hear their argument well but the body language implied there was some kind of disagreement. Then there was the shouting. The other man threw a punch. Matt deflected it. Punched him. The guy took a second to recover, then punched Matt again. And he went over the side of the boat and into the inlet. Timber started to attack, but he shot her and she went overboard, and somehow managed to make it back to shore."

Lily felt the emotional impact like a fist to her own throat, robbing her of breath. She could imagine the scene, the darkness of the sky and the even darker water. The splash as Matt went over, maybe the struggle to stay afloat in the murky, silty water. Or maybe not, maybe he'd been knocked unconscious immediately and hadn't had a chance at all. Either way, the image was clear of the water just swallowing him up, and the Alaskan tide carrying him away and out to sea never to be heard from again.

It was wrong, that was all there was to it. Even if maybe their relationship hadn't been the best, even if they'd had problems. Everyone did, right? And no one deserved to die like that. No one.

A sob welled up and escaped her throat, and unexpected tears made their way down her face.

"Lily?"

Travis's concern was appreciated, but it was almost too much. She felt over-whelmed, her head building with the pressure that was all her emotions swell-ing together inside her. "I… I wanted to know, thanks. I'm just thinking."

Thinking. Thinking. Thinking. She'd done entirely too much of that, and now here she was, stuck again on a July night an entire year ago when her life had changed.

Or had it changed then? Had it changed before, when Matt suggested she spend less time with friends and more time with him? Or had it changed when he told her the faith she'd been raised with was silly?

No, it was ridiculous not to remember the good times. The way he'd made her laugh. His smile. He'd died in the line of duty, died a hero.

Still, it was too much all threaded together in knots that Lily hadn't been able to untangle yet, no matter how many therapy sessions she'd been to, how many lattes she drank, how many positive social media posts she looked at.

Matt and her relationship had been deeply flawed.

He'd been murdered.

She mourned his loss every single day.

She mourned the loss of who she used to be, both before she lost him and even before their relationship.

"I think… I need a run. I think that'll help." She scooted her chair back from the table.

"I'll get my shoes," Travis said, moving quickly.

She shook her head. "No need, I don't think. Nothing weird happened at work today. Maybe he's given up."

Not that she believed that. Who would? She just couldn't fit one more thing in her mind right now, and she knew without a doubt that she needed to run, to feel the physical release of some of this tension. Besides, Timber had spent her day on a dog bed in the coffee shop, so she needed exercise, too.

"I'm coming anyway."

She thought she heard him say it, but

like a sleepwalker, she barely registered his words. She simply moved toward the front door and outside.

It still wasn't too late, and there was plenty of daylight. See? She'd be fine. Never mind that daylight hadn't kept her safe yesterday.

"Timber, come." She looked around the clearing for anything out of place, but seeing nothing, started to run, Timber beside her.

Almost immediately, she could breathe easier, and her chest started to loosen. How was she supposed to explain her agony to Travis if he asked? Would he understand that it was possible to miss someone who had maybe hurt you?

Well, of course the answer to that was yes, she realized as soon as she wondered, but her situation was different.

Therapy had helped her understand that her relationship with Matt was not the healthiest, but she'd started to more fully accept that now that she was spending all this time with Travis, subconsciously comparing them. Was that fair to Travis, though? Or to Matt? How could she hold anything against someone who wasn't here anymore? And why did grief have to be such a complicated knot?

There wasn't a distance she could run that would make this simpler, Lily knew that, but somehow she had to try. Or at least try to calm herself down as much as she could.

She wanted to take the trail in the woods behind Travis's house, but it didn't seem wise. She was foolish to venture out on her own at all, she was realizing as her head got clearer, even if Timber was a good protector. But she wasn't foolish enough to run on the dark, narrow paths back there. Instead she ran alongside the road, which did have some houses on it, though most appeared to be tucked back into their own little patches of woods.

She glanced behind her but didn't see Travis anywhere. Just when she'd started to hope that he had followed her against her wishes.

Didn't that just sum everything up? Did she wish Travis had pursued her even when she told him they were finished all those years ago? That would be absurd, she knew, but maybe part of her had hoped that.

It would have saved her from all the failure that had happened in the intervening years. That stupid list she'd had of dreams she wanted to chase before she got married… She thought of it now and wondered if Travis realized that of all the dreams she'd left their relationship to pursue, she'd only actually accomplished one. She had her own coffee shop. Everything else… Well, dreams were for kids, that was what Matt had told her when she'd tried to push him

away with the list, telling him a relationship wasn't on the list until last.

At the time, it had seemed romantic
that a man was willing to say, *Hey, but
what about me?* And so she'd ended up
with Matt. When really she'd missed
Travis the whole time.

Lily sped up her pace. What was wrong
with her?

She slowed slightly when she saw that
Timber was panting. "Sorry, girl. I have
a lot of feelings, I guess."

Timber's dark eyes were empathetic
but also seemed to imply that she appreciated the slower pace.

Taking a deep breath, Lily slowed all
the way to a walk, took a deep breath in
and let it out, and relaxed her shoulders.
She needed to go back to the house and
explain all of this to Travis. *All* of it, because what was the worst that could happen? He could reject her? She'd already
done that to him. Maybe it was fair to

even the playing field, let him experience what it was like.

The annoying fact was, she probably still loved Travis, definitely more than she loved herself. But she hadn't wanted to hurt him, because of that.

Her mom had hurt her when she left.

Definitely not something Lily wanted to dwell on. Her mom's abandonment of their family when Lily was in middle school had escalated her dad's drinking problem, and it had showed Lily that if you had dreams to chase, you'd better do it before you got married and had a family, because otherwise what if you just…abandoned them?

She hadn't wanted to do that. So she'd broken it off with Travis. She'd never really been able to explain to him why.

Picking her pace up again, she decided she should tell Travis that, too. Again, what was the worst that could happen? Maybe it was time for unguarded honesty.

Enjoying the stretch of her muscles, Lily turned back toward the house, narrowing the distance between herself and Travis with Timber at her side.

Then she heard the first gunshot.

Even with all the danger yesterday, her first thought was that a car had backfired. Something, anything besides a gunshot.

But then the gravel of the road flew up about ten feet in front of her. There were woods on either side. Someone was... shooting from the woods?

Being out in the open was now an awful feeling.

Her stomach churned. Which way was the shooting coming from? Left or right? She sprinted forward, praying for the first time in years and hoping that God was actually paying attention to her. Travis seemed to still take that for granted, like a fact, and he was an adult. Maybe that was another one of those things her relationship with Matt had changed that she needed to change back.

Either way, God seemed to be her only option at the moment.

"Please help me figure this out. Please don't let Timber get hit, or me, either," she muttered under her breath as she ran, trying her best to be aware of her surroundings.

The only way she'd be able to pinpoint a location any better would be if they shot again, though she certainly didn't want...

Another shot. This time, judging by the way the gravel shot up, she was fairly certain they were on her left. The side of the road Travis's house was on.

"Timber, ready?" She gave the dog the signal that a command was coming, then dove off the road and rolled down the slope into the woods. She darted through the trees, glancing down now and then to make sure Timber was still with her. The dog's demeanor seemed to have changed, as if she could sense that something was wrong.

Lily heard another shot. So they were following her. She'd still have to run, and somehow she'd have to get back to Travis.

"Really, God, I'm going to need Your help here, I think," she admitted out loud as she ran. "If You're really involved, please, please show up here and keep me safe. I'll try not to do anything stupid after this if You do."

And Lily ran, praying and hoping beyond hope that she'd get to tell Travis all the things she wanted to say.

Travis didn't understand why Lily hadn't waited for him. He'd watched the emotions chase across her face and understood that she was probably feeling more than she was ready to admit. Should he have pulled punches a little more, tried to ease the blow of what had actually happened that night a year ago?

He didn't think so. It gave him no pleasure to know that he'd said something to hurt and overwhelm her, but he cared too much about Lily not to treat her respectfully. To him, that meant telling her the whole story.

He ran faster than he would prefer along the trails in the woods. No sign of Lily. He'd been running about five minutes when he wondered if she'd have gone along the road instead. She always preferred trail running, but like he'd been trying to remind himself, people did change. He reversed his direction, passed by his house and went out onto the main road. He couldn't see her, but the way his road twisted and turned, he probably wouldn't be able to.

He'd been running for over a mile when he heard what sounded like a gunshot. Forget *sounded like*—it was a gunshot.

Resisting the urge to scream her name, knowing that could put her in even more danger, he sprinted ahead. Another shot. A third.

They weren't close together, he comforted himself with that. It wasn't rapid-fire as though someone was being gunned down. More like a hunter had been lying in wait for something and was finally taking his chance. The fact that there had been more than one shot was good, right? Probably Lily hadn't gone down with the first? And Timber? Timber had to be okay. Lily was his top priority, of course, but he loved that dog.

At times like this, he was thankful that he didn't believe in an indifferent God, the way Lily had talked about earlier. No matter what, Travis knew that God was right there, present with him, extremely involved. He prayed now, believing God would rescue them.

And he ran. If he was going to help Lily, he was going have to catch her.

At first he stuck to the road, and then something urged him toward the woods on the other side of the road. It was illogical. Surely if Lily was trying to get back to his house, the woods on the correct side of the road would be preferable. But on the other hand, if someone was stalking her, having followed her from his house…

Trusting God and his instincts, Travis continued to run. Until he nearly ran straight into Lily.

Grabbing her by the shoulders to brace her as he couldn't slow down, he whispered immediately, "You okay?" He checked her quickly for any signs of injury.

"Yes. You?"

He nodded, then looked down at Timber. "She's all right, too?"

Lily's nod reassured him again.

"We need to get out of here," he said, stating the obvious.

"How do you propose we do that?"

He thought for a second, then smiled. "I've got a plan."

NINE

Waiting out a shooter in the woods had not been in Lily's plans for the night, but here they were. Travis, being familiar with these woods, knew where there was a thick patch of alders, and they'd gotten down on their knees and crawled into the curtain of branches they provided. It wasn't the sturdiest of hideouts, which made her uncomfortable, but it was better than running through the woods blind, not knowing where the shooter was.

"You doing okay?" Travis whispered. They were both sitting on the ground, their arms brushing against each other. Lily tried to tell herself that she was finding it difficult to breathe because of stress, but she wasn't entirely sure it didn't have more to do with his closeness.

"I'm ready to be inside somewhere," Lily replied nervously.

"It's probably safe to talk, as long as we're quiet and Timber isn't on alert."

Her eyes went to Timber, who was lying on Lily's other side. Lily could just make out her shape in the fading light.

Lily knew Travis was right, that this was a good plan. The sky had stayed daylight for hours and hours, and they'd sat mostly in silence. Now, though, the sky was gradually darkening to a denim blue. Soon, they'd be able to move through the woods relatively undetected.

Of course, that meant that whoever was after her would be able to also. Lily reached down and petted Timber, needing to calm her anxiety.

"So..." Lily trailed off. Everything

she'd meant to say had seemed like such a good idea earlier, when she was running, and maybe an ever better idea after that, when she'd been afraid for her life and wondering if she was always going to regret the way things had ended between her and Travis. Sitting here beside him now was a little different. He wasn't just a concept from her past, he was a living, breathing person who could… reject her.

It had sounded so much easier when talking had been theoretical.

"So?" he said in return, and it sounded encouraging. Maybe she could do this after all.

"I was thinking earlier… Man, there's so much to say."

He shifted so he was facing her somewhat. Their arms were still touching, but his face was only inches from hers now, studying her.

Lily looked down, then back up at him.

"You know my mom left when I was in middle school."

He nodded, and Lily thought his expression may have darkened. The two of them had known each other back then, but they hadn't been anywhere near as close as they would be in high school. "I never really knew why," she went on, "until I was in high school. I found a letter from her when I was looking through my baby pictures for our senior yearbook."

"What did she say?" His voice sounded as tight as her chest felt right now.

"She, uh, she said she had to leave. That she hadn't pursued her dreams before getting married and starting a family and regretted it, so…" The words tumbled out all at once. "So she left us. I guess maybe that's why I couldn't get married. No, wait." Lily cleared her throat. "I'm not doing this well. I know that's why I was afraid to get married after high school. It wasn't you, or any-thing you did, it was entirely me. I didn't want to end up like my mom."

He didn't say anything for a couple of minutes. Lily thought maybe it had gone better than she could have hoped. Either way, at least it was over now.

"But you fixed it by doing the same thing."

"What?"

"You did the same thing she did. I mean, it's not the exact same, we weren't a family. But you're saying that you didn't want to hurt me, so you just left to chase your dreams so…what? So you wouldn't do the exact same thing later?"

Never, *never* had anyone compared Lily to her mom. Well, not since after middle school anyway when her mom's name couldn't be said in the house with-out her dad reaching for the Jack Dan-iels. And Lily had never wanted to be like her.

How could Travis say that?

Emotions rubbed raw, Lily grappled to even articulate exactly what she was feeling. Frustration? Anger?

Hurt. Deep hurt. From her mom, from Travis.

Why had she thought it was a good idea to be honest with him? Now she saw the situation for what it was. She'd showed him her heart, and he'd shoved her away, pointing out the areas with scars and shortcomings. As if she still wasn't haunted by fears that she could one day end up like her mom, he'd thrown it in her face that she was.

The longer she sat in her quiet anger, the more upset she got.

"Lily? You okay?"

How many times had he asked her that over the past few days? But this time, she truly was not.

"Actually I'm not super great, which

makes sense given what you just said to me."

At least one of her thoughts on her run had been true, and that was that she didn't need to care what he thought anymore. Honesty wasn't just the best policy in this case; it was the only one that made any sense.

She studied his face for any hint of malice or intentional cruelty but found none. Odd since the words he'd said so carelessly had been so effective at shattering her heart.

"I didn't meant to hurt your feelings," he began.

Listening to him fumble through an apology he may or may not really mean wasn't high on her list of things to do. "Just stop. Please."

If anyone could hear them now it would be almost comical, the way they were whispering so seriously. Of course, with the tension between them thicker than the growing darkness, any bit of the comical was welcome, at least to Lily's way of thinking.

"I don't want to walk away from uncomfortable conversations, Lily. We're working together for who knows how long. I don't want there to be stuff between us."

Wasn't there already too much between them for that to ever be true? Their history was half a decade of hurt. So many shared dreams, and then her dreams had ultimately destroyed what they'd had together. It seemed so ironic now, when she considered how few of those dreams she'd left their relationship for had actually come true. She'd had so many big plans and ideas, but life had intervened. At some point she'd met Matt, and he'd convinced her to walk away from the rest of her dreams.

And now here she was. The owner of a coffee shop, which she was very proud of, but also she was very much alone and felt purposeless, like her future was just one endless sea of beige. Where was the adventure she'd longed for? Had she played life too safe? Or...had she taken the wrong risks?

She met Travis's eyes, saw the usual warm kindness in them and realized that no matter how hurt she felt, or how offended she might be tempted to be, he was telling the truth. He truly hadn't meant to hurt her.

"You saying I was like my mom hurt," she finally said. "But I can see why it seemed like that to you. I don't know... I don't know. I haven't thought about that enough." Her voice broke a little.

"I really didn't mean to upset you. I'm glad you told me, honestly. I always wondered why. I thought we were good. Kinda thought we were, you know, the real deal and then..." He trailed off, but she knew how the story ended. She'd lived it.

Maybe she wasn't the only one who was hurt. She should remember that.

Sitting in the grove of alders, the darkness the only real protection they had, Travis's every sense was already on alert. And that was before Lily dropped the bomb that she'd dumped him because she hadn't wanted to be like her mom.

He hadn't meant to hurt her. He'd told her the truth, but he understood why it had hurt. And he was sorry.

Without thinking, he reached over, grabbed her hand and squeezed it lightly, like he'd done so many times through the years.

Only then did his mind catch up with his emotions and scream for him to stop. He'd already been rejected once. If anyone was in danger of getting hurt, it was certainly him.

But now he already had her hand. What was he going to do, pull away? That would invite more questions. Better to play it cool but keep it in his head that Lily wasn't someone who'd be happy with a regular life. She wanted adventures, she wanted the things on that list. And she should have them.

Or maybe she already did? She'd been engaged, which was at the end of her list. That would make more sense.

"So you get all those dreams accomplished?" He tried to keep his voice light and undemanding. Still, he could feel himself holding his breath as he waited for her answer.

But instead of the assured yes he'd been expecting, she tensed beside him, and he knew he'd said the wrong thing again.

"Unfortunately no. Life is weird, right?"

She laughed, but it was hollow and humorless.

"You didn't give up on them, did you?"

She shrugged, and he understood immediately that the answer was yes. Somehow without being told, he suspected his no-nonsense partner had something to do with that.

"So what happened?" he asked.

"Everything and nothing. I did open the coffee shop, but then I realized how many of my dreams conflicted. I mean, really? I was going to be a small business owner but also manage to travel and explore new places? I don't know what I was thinking."

Travis remembered the list. He'd been really proud of her in high school when she'd showed it to him and told him about her dreams. Once upon a time, he'd thought maybe he would even help her accomplish some of them, but that obviously hadn't been the case.

"You were a kid, and the sky was the limit."

"So ignorant."

"Hopeful. I prefer to think of it as hopeful," he corrected.

"Anyway," she continued, "nothing happened, I just grew up. And then I met Matt, and we started dating, and when he wanted to get more serious, he pointed out that my idea about finishing this list before I went on with my life was kind of childish. So I thought he was right and…forgot about it."

The way her voice hesitated on the word *forgot* told him that she most certainly had not forgotten about it.

"Remind me what all was on this list."

"Silly things, Travis."

"What else do we have to do right now, though, besides silly stuff?"

She seemed to be weighing her options. "Fine." And she shifted beside him. Closer? Travis didn't know. He'd been distracted by her proximity since they'd climbed into the makeshift natural shelter.

"First, I was going to open my own coffee shop, so I'd have a job."

"Which you did, and it's fantastic."

"Had you been before today?"

He nodded. "Several times. I just—" he looked away "—I used to try to go when you weren't out front working the register." He'd wanted to support her but hadn't wanted to cause any kind of drama.

It seemed like she took a minute to process that and then nodded. "That was really sweet of you."

"What else was on the list?"

She shrugged, laughing softly at herself. "A couple of things, I—" She stopped.

When Travis looked over at her, she was staring at Timber, who was focused on something out in the distance, her body tense.

Sometimes it was frustrating not to have the senses of a dog, because Travis couldn't hear anything. He didn't think Lily could, either, though she had her eyes closed and seemed to be focusing all her energy into hearing whatever her dog had.

Timber lowered her head slightly. For a second, her lip curled back.

Travis felt for the handgun he had in his waistband holster. They weren't defenseless, for which he was thankful, but he knew Lily had already been through a lot. Another shootout wasn't something she needed. He made himself sit still, waiting. Lily did the same.

After one minute, maybe two, which stretched out in a seemingly endless silence, Timber laid her head back down, her muscles gradually relaxing.

It seemed they were safe again, for now.

"Maybe we should go?" Lily whispered.

Travis immediately nodded. It was dark enough to give them cover, and he wasn't willing to risk sitting here waiting for someone to find them. "We'll finish this conversation later."

"We don't have to do that," she protested.

Travis put his hands on her upper arms and turned her gently till she faced him. "I want to, Lily," he said, eyes meeting hers. It felt like there was some kind of bond between them that time hadn't managed to break, not completely. If anything, it was more obvious to Travis now than when he'd been younger that there was something between them, and maybe there always would be.

Thinking of her safety and the unknown threats that could still be lurking in the woods, he made himself look away from her. Nodding in the direction of his house, he said, "Let's go. We need to get you back home and safe."

"I don't even have a home," she mumbled.

"Maybe the fire department will call tomorrow. But you're welcome in my cabin for as long as you need it," he told her as they crawled carefully out of the alders.

As though by mutual consent, once they left the shelter of the trees, neither of them talked. Travis found his senses heightened as he looked between the dark shapes of spruce and birch trees. The sky was a deep blue, not quite black—it still wouldn't be fully dark for long at all this early in July—but the midnight twilight allowed them some shelter to get back to the house.

Timber seemed to understand what they were trying to do, and she kept a steady pace in front of both of them, keeping her nose up and sniffing the air.

It was reassuring to know that she was using her skills to scan the woods for them; at least they could confirm that they were fairly safe.

Travis was always thankful that Timber hadn't been killed in the attack that had taken Matt's life, but never more so than now. It was like having another officer at his side, except one who had super heightened senses and didn't hog the coffee.

It didn't take long for them to make their way through the woods, even at the careful pace they'd set, and soon they were approaching Travis's house.

"Any chance you've got more hot chocolate?" she asked Travis.

He laughed, the tension from the night demanding some release. "You know I do."

"Yeah, I was pretty sure." She hurried inside and into his kitchen.

Travis followed, giving Timber a rewarding pat as she went by him into the house.

Making the hot chocolate was easy enough, he thought, as he topped a couple of mugs with whipped cream and sprinkles. The problem was calming down enough to drink it.

It was all starting to slam into him now. Lily had really been shot at. Her life had been in danger. Again. Then the conversation in the shelter of the trees, in the dark…

Something about talking in the dark made everything feel so much less guarded. Lily hadn't stopped loving him, or at least that wasn't why she'd broken up with him at graduation. There was something deeply reassuring about that; her leaving so suddenly all those years ago had made him question so many things he'd known to be true. This made so much more sense. It didn't change what had happened, but it sure made it easier to deal with.

"You're sure you don't need to get checked out? No bruises, no injuries at all?" He looked her over the best he could in a respectful way, but Lily shook her head.

"He shot at me a couple of times, but it wasn't ever as close as it could have been."

"Bad shot or intentional misses?" he asked aloud, not knowing if he was really looking for an answer.

Lily shrugged. "I'm not sure."

Travis carried the hot chocolates into the living room, and Lily followed, exactly as they'd done the night before. Travis felt that he could get used to this, having a nightly hot cocoa with Lily. Except...that wasn't what she needed, was it?

As he set their drinks down onto the coffee table, it all seemed so clear to him. Matt had encouraged her to stop dreaming, stop pursuing her list; Travis was fairly sure he'd understood that correctly. What Lily really needed was a friend, someone who would encourage her to follow those dreams. Even if doing so would mean she returned to the line of thinking that she couldn't be in a relationship till she accomplished more.

Still, it would be worth it to help her, because he knew it was what Lily wanted. And he really loved seeing her smile.

"Come tell me about the rest of that list. Where were we before we got interrupted?"

He was rewarded by her easy smile. Travis took a long sip of cocoa and waited for Lily to share some of her other dreams.

TEN

"You're sure you want to talk about this? Like I said, it's silly. Ridiculous even."

"I honestly don't think I'll see it that way," Travis said.

Lily believed him. She hadn't thought it was that bad of a list of dreams until Matt had seemed so down on it. Was it somewhat unrealistic? Sure. But wasn't dreaming part of being alive? Maybe that was why the last year of grief hadn't felt quite as jarring as she'd expected it to. In some ways, she hadn't been fully alive in years, not since…well, not since walking away from who she was in exchange for a relationship.

That had been the heart of the problem with her and Matt, she realized. She had given up too much. And maybe he had, too? But love wasn't supposed to make you change who you were, right? It was supposed to make you a better version, maybe. At least, that was the gist she'd gotten from countless books and TV shows.

"Okay. If you're sure…" She took a breath. "I also wanted plenty of things that didn't make sense."

"Like?"

"I was going to travel a lot." She laughed. "It sounded fun. I wanted to go to Europe, hike around… I wanted to learn another language first, of course, so that I could converse with people."

"Oh, yeah? Which?"

"I was flexible there. French seemed practical. German. Maybe Norwegian. I was also going to learn some new hobbies." She shrugged. "Stuff like that."

There had been more, but it felt strange and oddly personal to talk about. Lily wasn't sure she wanted to go into any more detail. Still, she appreciated that he cared. Looking at him now, it was clear that he had really been listening.

"And you decided you didn't want to get married?" Travis's voice was careful as he asked the question, and Lily could imagine why.

How weird must it be for him to know that she'd walked away from what they had because of this list, and yet she'd agreed to marry Matt? Admittedly, it seemed inconsistent.

"No, it just wasn't on the list because it was assumed. I always wanted to get married and have a family, but I figured I should do the other things first. Get them out of the way, sort of. Have my life together."

Not like her mom. She could tell that he heard the unspoken words, too.

"It just seemed like what was best," she finished.

A heavy silence surrounded them in a way that was impossible to ignore. She'd made her choices, and now she had to live with them. Losing Travis wasn't something that had happened to her like she was a victim. She'd broken them up. She'd made other choices. She didn't have any right to go back on those now.

Even if he did make fantastic hot chocolate and listen to her better than anyone ever had.

She took another sip of the warm drink, letting the liquid warm her throat, her chest, her heart. When was the last time she'd just sat down and talked to someone else like this? She'd missed this kind of closeness. She had liked that about being with Matt—she'd had someone to talk to on a regular basis.

She and Travis had always had this

kind of easy relationship, where they could sit and talk and just be together for hours. She'd tried to duplicate it, but no one else had ever been Travis.

The thought was terrifying. She'd never bought into the idea of soul mates and having one person who was right for you, but what if it was true? What if Travis had been her one chance, and she'd messed it up?

Lily's eyes stung with tears she absolutely would not shed. As much as all the things on her list meant to her, she'd always wanted a family and someone to share her life with. Had she forfeited that? She certainly hoped not.

Much as she hated the awkward silence, she didn't know what to say. Out there in the woods, telling him everything had seemed like such a good idea. He knew now, at least, that their breakup hadn't been because of anything he'd done. He'd been the best boyfriend she could have hoped for, and while they'd had their arguments like any normal couple, it had also been so easy between them.

Not able to stand it anymore, Lily stood up. "I've got to do something."

"You just got shot at, don't you think that's enough excitement for the night?"

He had a point, even though his eyes were sparkling... Wait, was he seriously teasing her?

It warmed her chest every bit as much as the hot chocolate, and Lily felt some of her internal chaos relax.

"Was Matt really killed randomly? Could it have been anyone who died that night? Or was he closer than anyone else to figuring out who was involved... or...or something? What if we walked through it all together?" She'd read enough mystery books to throw ideas out, but realistically she knew very little about what would be needed to conduct an actual investigation.

"We assumed it was just because he was involved. Maybe he said something that night that made them realize he was arresting them? There was no way to find out. The trail went cold the second he..."

"Went overboard," Lily finished for him, the words stinging less than they had earlier in the night. There was no driving need to go run this time.

Travis nodded.

"What was the investigation like immediately after? I mean, did APD check out his apartment or..." She tried to remember what had been done at the time. Matt's personal affairs hadn't been hers to handle, since they'd been engaged and hadn't lived together. He'd paid rent months in advance... Was it possible he still had the apartment leased?

"We looked around the apartment.

Nothing was out of place. It was extremely clean."

"Huh. Matt wasn't the neatest, but that's good, I guess. Other than that, there wasn't anything useful there?" she asked.

"I think there are photos in this file somewhere." Travis nodded to the stack they'd been going through earlier. "But we can wait, Lily. None of this has to be done right now."

People had said the same thing to her after Matt's death. But the truth was things did have to be done. Sometimes it was easier just to buckle down and get through them.

"I think I'm better now," she said.

Travis stood, got the stack of files from the table and brought them back to the couch. "Mind if I sit here?" he asked, motioning to the spot next to her.

"No, for sure, that's fine." Belatedly, Lily realized that a handful of words spilling out of her mouth instead of a simple *no* probably betrayed the fact that his proximity did shake her up at least a bit.

In any case, he did sit down beside her.

"Yeah, here they are." He pulled a stack of printed photos out of the pile. "Nothing interesting that we found."

No matter how certain Lily had been that she was ready to wade back into this, the photos of Matt's apartment did throw her a little. First of all it was so familiar. She'd spent so much time there when they first started dating. Even if their time together had diminished at the end, probably due to how invested he'd been in the narcotics case, they'd had some good times in that apartment.

She'd watched some of her favorite movies on that couch, listening to Matt mumble about how action movies were better than chick flicks. She'd tried to watch some with him, but her taste in action movies only ran as far as Jack Ryan, a classic hero who never sought out heroism. Matt tended to like the flashier movies. He was more of a Tom Cruise than a Harrison Ford.

Travis was right that the apartment was very clean. Matt had always been more of a *leave his boots in the middle of the floor and get them later* kind of guy, but these photos didn't look like that at all. Even the trash cans were emptied.

"Have you ever noticed before how eerie it is to look at photos of someone's place after they're gone?" Lily turned to Travis to ask.

He nodded like he knew what she meant exactly, and she relaxed, appreciating being understood.

"This isn't like that." Lily continued, "I mean, it is, but in a different way. It just… It doesn't look like he was planning to come back."

Lily looked over at Travis again and

blinked as their eyes met. She spoke again. "That's exactly what's weird to me. It was rarely this clean. Do you think he knew it was going to go wrong?"

It had been a year, but she could feel her mind struggling to rewind to the last time she'd seen Matt. They'd argued about something stupid, she remembered. Where to go eat, maybe? Had he given any indication that he'd somehow known his death was coming?

No. Not that she could think of. He'd been off, stressed, shorter tempered than usual, but not depressed or giving any indication that he thought something awful was going to happen to him. No extra-long goodbyes, nothing.

But why was the apartment so clean?

She shook her head. "I hate that the further we look into this, the more questions I have. I keep thinking if I just take a deep breath, focus on it one more time, then maybe I'll understand. Maybe I'll be able to really move on."

"Is it his death that's keeping you from that, though?" Travis asked.

Lily frowned. "What do you mean?"

"Your list, your mom…"

Lily flinched.

"Are you sure you aren't keeping yourself from moving forward? Do you know what you want moving forward to look like?"

It was the stupidest question she'd ever heard. She, who had daydreamed her way through several high school classes and written a to-do list that haunted her in more ways than one, not moving forward? She'd always been able to dream about her future and make plans and now…

Now she had the coffee shop. She dreamed of one day running the shop without the weight of the grief she felt over Matt, but…her dreams were all just focused on getting things back to how they used to be.

What was Travis saying? That she needed a new dream?

Would solving this case somehow help like Lily thought it would, or was Travis right? Was she the one keeping herself stuck?

He'd overstepped, Travis knew it, and he wasn't sure how he was going to get out of this one.

Lily was looking at him, her eyes wide, blinking.

It seemed like it was too late to *put down the shovel* as his mom had always said, so he kept talking. "What do you want, Lily? Like, really, what do you want?"

She stared at him as though he was the answer.

And in slow motion, like her gaze was pulling her toward him, Travis felt himself drawn closer to her. Or was she moving toward him? Either way, it was like an invisible force, slow but determined. Her eyes were still, beautiful pools of blue.

"Lily?"

"Yeah?" Her whisper pulled him even closer.

"I'm going to kiss you if you don't back up." His breathing had quickened, and he could feel his heart beating in his chest. Was he really going to do this? Had he really said that?

She moved closer, and he had his answer for both questions.

Like someone who had returned from a long journey and wasn't sure of whether home was really theirs anymore, he brushed her lips gently with his, another question.

She answered with more pressure.

Travis found him kissing her fully, without thinking, lips moving over hers in a way that was not at all familiar, no matter how many times they'd done this in the past. This was new, fresh. And it meant more to him than the one hundred kisses they'd shared as high schoolers.

Lily was complicated, and Travis knew his life had been simpler before she'd called him just a few days ago, but he didn't need simple. He'd asked her what her dreams for the future were, but he hadn't really been asking himself.

The answer was this.

He ended the kiss far sooner than he wanted to, drawing back just enough to meet her eyes again.

"You. I want…" She swallowed hard. Looked away. "I want you, but… I don't know how to do this. How can you trust me again? How can I trust myself? What about all this, and Matt's death, and…" She stood up and walked across the room, and Travis felt her absence immediately. "What if it's just messed me up beyond repair? I can't do that to you."

He knew she'd changed, but he wanted to know this new version of her. Not just her lips. But her heart. Her dreams. "You're not."

"But how do you know?"

He could see one single tear chasing its way down her cheek.

She shook her head again. "I'm sorry, Travis."

His stomach tightened, knowing the rest of that sentence. She shouldn't have kissed him. Shouldn't want him.

Was he really so stupid that he would set himself up for rejection from the same woman multiple times? Part of his mind reminded him that it might not be him she was rejecting. She'd been though a lot. Tonight alone had been overwhelming.

"What's a kiss between friends, right? We're still friends, Lily."

"Friends."

She reached up and touched her lips, and Travis could almost feel the electricity. She knew it, too, even if neither of them was going to admit it. That had *not* been the kind of kiss two friends could share and shrug off. For Travis, that was the kind of kiss he could only experience with the woman who had been and apparently still was straight out of his dreams.

"We can be friends," she said, blowing out a long breath. "But we probably…"

"Yeah, shouldn't do that again," he finished for her. He patted the couch cushion beside him. "Want to come back, look at the file more?"

"Do you mind if we pick this back up tomorrow, after work?" She was already moving toward the back door, toward the guest cabin.

"You're going to need to talk to the police. We should have called them tonight." He'd sent a text to Officer Keller, the woman who'd come by yesterday— had that been only yesterday? He'd let her know that Lily had been shot at but asked if it was possible for her to talk to them the next day.

"Tomorrow... I will, after work. Sure." Lily reached for the doorknob. "Walk me back?"

He appreciated that she at least wasn't completely throwing safety to the wind, but he figured it would be better not to talk about anything serious as he walked her to the guest cabin. Instead he answered her questions about when he'd bought the property, his plans for the cabin, simple things like that. She seemed determined to get them back on level footing.

"Sleep well," he told her after establishing that no one else was inside the cabin. Timber, who had curled up at his house and taken a long nap, seemed alert and ready to be watchful.

Lily smiled back at him, and he felt like maybe they could pull this off. Maybe they could be friends.

"You, too, Travis."

His heart and breath caught at the same time, and he realized the truth. He was probably going to love Lily Peterson for the rest of his life.

Walking back to his house after he'd double-and triple-checked Lily's doors, Travis tried to decide if he had any hopes that she might change her mind about them. After all, she was under an extreme amount of stress, that was for sure.

But for now, he needed to respect her request to back off. Be friends.

What would a friend do?

He sat back down on his couch, wishing Lily was still there, and eyed the stack of papers. He didn't have a lot to offer her. At the moment, he didn't even have his own dreams totally lined up.

Being a police officer had always been it for him before Matt's death had driven him away. It had made him question if the good he could do was worth immersing himself in all the evil he saw on the job. Did good really win? Could evil be stopped?

He knew the answer according to the Bible, but that didn't mean it felt true when you were standing at someone's door telling them that because of someone else's bad choices, their fiancé wouldn't come home.

When he'd seen how much it had crushed Lily after someone had come to her door to tell her bad news, he decided he was never going to do it again. For the months he'd stayed at the department, he avoided it, and then realized that maybe it had broken him, too.

Maybe Lily wasn't the only one who felt messed up beyond repair.

Quitting his job hadn't solved anything, though. Here he was, face-to-face with that kind of evil and pain again, except this time without all the resources he'd had as a police officer.

Travis flipped through the file about Matt's death, reading enough to remind himself of other details he hadn't remembered, like interviews with Matt's acquaintances who reported that the case had been taking over his life. That, connected to the fact that Lily had been so surprised by how clean his apartment had been, bothered Travis. Bothered him enough that he got up off the couch and started doing sit-ups, partly to clear his mind and partly to see if he still could just in case maybe he wanted to go back to law enforcement. Maybe. One day.

Thirty sit-ups in, he'd confirmed his muscles were still in good shape even if his confidence wasn't, and he'd come to some conclusions that bothered him.

Something hadn't been right in that investigation. The signs had been there, but somehow he hadn't noticed, even though he'd been Matt's partner.

Matt hadn't...hadn't been working both sides, had he?

It felt disloyal to even consider. Travis weighed his options. Who could he talk to at the police department who knew enough about the case to be helpful processing it, but who wouldn't immediately take his thoughts as something that was truth? The last thing he wanted was to sully his friend's name after his death.

But what if his friend had been guilty? Didn't Lily deserve to know?

Would she want to know?

He stood up, paced some more, then went outside to patrol the property. He didn't go close to the cabin, not wanting to wake Timber, but he made sure nothing looked amiss.

When he went inside, questions about Matt still taunted him. He wasn't going to get much sleep tonight.

ELEVEN

"Can you get that, Hannah?"

The phone had been ringing more than usual today, Lily thought. It seemed like suddenly people she'd been trying to get ahold of for weeks about coffee shop business were all calling her back, making her normally busy workday more hectic than usual. Right now she was in the middle of making a customer's latte, and the espresso machine had been finicky earlier in the morning. The last thing she wanted was to have to repull shots.

Focusing on what she was doing, she was startled when she felt Hannah's gentle tap on her shoulder.

"Sorry, I didn't mean to scare you."

Hannah frowned at her. "I guess I understand why you were scared, though, with everything going on."

So she'd heard about that. Lily had been hoping somehow the town was going to be oblivious to what she was going through.

"Anyway, the fire department is on the phone for you."

"Can you..." Lily gestured to the espresso machine where she had paper cups in a line waiting.

Hannah nodded, and Lily smiled an apology at the customer currently in line and walked to the phone.

"Lily Peterson speaking."

"Lily, it's Captain Caldwell from the Silvertip Creek Fire Department, how are you?"

"Fairly well, considering," she said.

"Your house has been cleared." He cut right to the chase. "It's structurally sound, so I don't see why you couldn't move back in immediately. The study where the fire was localized did sustain some damage, but nothing that caused loss of structural integrity. I would recommend you hire someone to clean that room."

Or she could do it herself, which would be infinitely cheaper. It wasn't that she was hurting of money, per se, but this dream of opening her own business hadn't come cheap. She wasn't exactly seeing the fruits of her business in excess yet.

"I can handle that. No problem."

They talked for a few more minutes about logistical details, and the captain left her with instructions that she should call if there was anything at all out of the ordinary when she got home.

It was almost too good to be true. She couldn't quite believe it. She was going home!

A shadow dimmed her excitement.

What if the man after her came back, and she was alone? It had been scary enough yesterday when she knew Travis was nearby. She couldn't imagine how terrifying it would be to be farther away from him.

But staying at Travis's house was a nonstarter. She'd still be alone in his guest cabin, technically, and while she knew it was different being so close to him and knowing he could be there any second, she was ultimately still alone either way. And she wasn't willing to be away from home forever.

Mind settled, she texted Travis. She did her best to sound reassuring, even as she wondered if the fire department had really thought this through. Or maybe they hadn't talked to the police department? Somehow she doubted the officers assigned to her case would be thrilled with the idea of her being alone.

Still, though, she was an adult and no

one had ordered her to stay at Travis's place or anything like that. She'd go home because that was what made the most sense.

And because she didn't know how she was going to sort out her feelings with him so close.

"Everything okay?" Hannah asked.

This time, Lily couldn't even rustle up a fake smile. "You know...long day."

Hannah raised her eyebrows like she didn't believe her. "What else is going on?"

Besides being hunted by a homicidal lunatic and being kissed so well by her former boyfriend that she forgot everything except the fact that maybe it wasn't too late for a future? With Travis, she didn't feel broken. Not that he *completed* her, Lily didn't feel that way at all, but she did like him and wasn't afraid to admit their attraction was still there. But she felt like a whole person, like someone whose flaws or griefs or struggles did not define her.

She felt safe. She felt known.

It was clear to her that she needed to get out of his house. Had he bought her comment about being friends? In some ways, friendship was the last thing she could imagine when that kiss had been everything she wanted and more. But Lily couldn't trust herself right now. Her emotions were overwhelmed with this case and the threat against her. Travis Beckett had been hard enough to get over the first time—she had no desire to repeat the experience.

"Uh...nothing," she finally said, her mind still a million miles away.

Hannah's expression implied that she knew Lily wasn't telling the entire truth, but she graciously let it go. "I got all those drinks made. I was thinking, do you want me to close up today?"

Usually Hannah opened, and Lily

closed. But she would love to go home and assess how bad things were at her house. She needed to see if she could move in tonight or if she would need to pick up some things.

And then there was her plan to go out with Travis and survey some of the areas near where Matt had died, just to see if they could get a clearer picture of what had gone on that night and why. There had to be some detail they were missing.

"I think I'll take you up on that," Lily said at last. "See you tomorrow."

Hannah waved, and Lily grabbed her purse and headed out the door. She was reaching for the handle of her car door when her phone rang. Travis.

"Hey, what's up?" she asked.

"The fire department just called me to let me know that your house was okay."

"They just called me, too. I wonder why they called you?"

"I have a buddy who works there."

Of course he did. Travis was so well connected in the law enforcement/rescue/public service world.

"I want to go over and check it out," she said, "but do you want to do that first or check out the bluffs?"

"Tonight?" Travis asked.

"Well, today, but yeah. I thought I'd leave the shop early."

He didn't say anything for a while, and Lily felt like she was being measured. She stood up straight, as if that would help her project strength through the phone call. Everything in her wanted to ignore yesterday. She didn't want to go over what had happened with the gunshots and being trapped in the woods. She just wanted to move on.

"You're sure you should?" Travis said at last. "I can do this alone."

He didn't sound like he was mocking or even pitying her, which would have been worse, but the words still chafed.

"Yeah, I'm good. I'm fine."

"Okay. I'll meet you at the overlook?"

Lily agreed, got in her car and drove away from the shop and out of town.

The overlook Travis had mentioned was the parking lot at the trailhead that led down to the edge of the inlet. The silty mudflats could be fatal if a person got stuck in them. About once a year, someone would venture into the mud-flats and need to be rescued. It was the closet thing to quicksand that Lily knew of. If the texture was just right, it could suck a person in and refuse to let them out.

They'd have to be careful while they investigated. Lily wouldn't be able to forgive herself if something happened to Travis because of her.

Travis hadn't been to the bluff over Knik Arm in months now. In the months after Matt's death, Travis found himself there often, sitting on one of the benches near the parking lot or wandering down toward the water itself, careful to steer clear of the mudflats and the metal-colored water. Some days it was fairly calm, but today he could see the currents churning. The water looked restless.

Travis could relate.

Kissing Lily had been incredible. He should have known she was going to backpedal from it, but it still hurt a little. How could things between them be so perfect and so impossible at the same time?

He climbed out of his car and waited for Lily to pull up. Within a minute or two, she arrived, and he watched as she opened the door of her car. He tensed as she made her way across the empty parking lot, an easy target in the massive open space.

He'd called both Anchorage PD and

Silvertip Creek PD today to get a feel for whether they had the manpower to put any kind of temporary bodyguard on Lily. They didn't, as he anticipated, though Silvertip Creek PD thought they might be able to have one of the patrol officers swing by her house more often.

Much as he didn't like the plan, Travis wasn't surprised that Lily was going to move back to her house now that the fire department had given her the go-ahead. Home mattered to her, for one thing, and for another, she didn't like to feel like an imposition.

He wished she felt as at home at his house as her own. He'd done his best to move on, had dated several times since high school, but he'd be lying if he didn't acknowledge that he still had some furnishings that he'd picked out with Lily in mind.

"Good day?" he asked her as she got

close. Timber followed them closely behind her.

Lily shook her head. "Too much going on."

"You don't have to go home right away, you know," he tried. "You could hire people to do the repair work, stay at the cabin..."

Lily was already shaking her head as though she'd expected this. She knew him well. "I have to go home, Travis. I can't live like this indefinitely."

There was a massive difference between what was likely to be just a few weeks and *indefinitely*. But he could see her point, especially with Matt's death on the verge of officially becoming a cold case. One year, and they'd learned little that they hadn't discovered in the first forty-eight hours after his death.

Maybe Travis was foolish to think they could uncover more.

"I get it." He reached for her hand as

they approached the narrow path down toward the inlet. "It's slick." And he didn't want her to feel like she was facing this alone, but figured the first reason was more acceptable to her.

Lily reached her hand out, and he held it in his, swallowing back emotion as he reminded himself that she wanted to be friends and that was it.

Much of his day at the hardware store had been spent thinking through that, in between helping customers. If she wanted to be friends, he could do that, but how could he be a really good friend to her? The question had circled his mind all day, and he'd finally landed on her list.

Could he help her complete it, at least somewhat? Maybe she couldn't travel the world, but could she travel around here?

He hated the idea of her feeling her life was incomplete, with something inside her begging to do more and see more, and her shutting it up just because society implied it was time for her to settle down. If Matt was alive, Travis would give him a good shove for talking Lily into thinking her dreams were silly.

Did Travis wish those dreams hadn't come between the two of them? Yes. But maybe now the best thing he could do for her was help her fulfill them.

"So where were you that night?" she asked when they were halfway down the narrow trail. Grass and other plants grew along the sides, but the middle was mud, worn down from use. No matter how often people were told the mud-flats were dangerous, they held a special allure. And this particular spot, where Matt's meetup had happened, was where the river was most accessible for people who liked to push the boundaries.

Everything looked different in daylight, especially a good six months after he'd been here last. That had been an oppressively gray winter day when he'd felt like hope was a concept that wasn't quite reachable. He'd come here, sat for a while in his grief with no real conclusions and then realized that sometimes life meant going on even without wrapping up the last chapter.

And he'd tried. Maybe even succeeded. Being here now felt like a step back and a step forward all at once.

"I was..." He looked around at the tall vegetation, the shape of the slope, the way the inlet angled below them where it cut into the bank. That was where the boat had been. Travis had had a nearly perfect visual, though he'd not been able to hear anything other than the rise and fall of voices. "There."

He pointed to a spot up ahead, on the left side of the trail. He'd spent time before what should have been the drug bust finding the best spot to hide and still be close enough to take quick action.

Travis walked toward where he'd been hiding but didn't go into the thick brush. Lily stayed beside him.

Timber's ears perked up.

She'd been with them that night. She'd stayed back with Travis while Matt boarded the boat and prepped for making the arrests. Travis had watched her flinch at a loud voice, though she stayed down as instructed. Together, they'd watched the scene unfold. Timber wasn't a stranger to this place, either. Perhaps she also wasn't a stranger to the grief that accompanied it.

Still, whatever reaction he'd been expecting from her, it wasn't this.

The fur on her scruff stiffened, and her eyes focused on the brush.

"Timber, stay," he said firmly.

Ignoring him, Timber crept forward.

Immediately Lily turned to him. "What is she doing?"

"I have no idea." He'd worked with Timber for years, and she'd been so reliable. This entire case was confusing— she wasn't behaving in a predictable way. Police dogs were supposed to be all but bombproof, always able to take commands. But this wasn't the first time it felt like Timber was operating entirely on her own. Travis struggled to find an explanation for her behavior, but nothing made sense.

She moved forward, not at a run, but purposefully.

"Let's follow her," he told Lily. They both trailed along behind the dog, making their way through the brush.

She was taking him right back to the spot he'd used as cover when he'd watched Matt's death go down one year ago.

How? Why?

His heart pounding, uncertainty roiling in his stomach, he followed her.

TWELVE

Lily had never understood all that Timber knew and was capable of, but it had struck her as strange how often Timber was running away from them. She was usually so obedient.

Now if she wasn't mistaken, Travis looked shaken up, too. Timber was trotting through the brush, near the direction where Travis had told her he'd hidden that night a year ago.

She hadn't considered what it would be like for him to come here. Was he okay? Or did it bring back memories in a way that overwhelmed him? Somehow she doubted that even if he did he would run off when someone was after him. She was able to see now how foolish that plan had been.

Up ahead, Timber stopped. Lily hurried to where she was and looked down at the ground.

It was still more cleared out in this spot than around it, though the brush seemed to have grown up somewhat. In several places, though, the earth was disturbed, and dirt was piled haphazardly, like someone had been digging for something.

"Did you…did you have to dig out a place to hide or something?" she asked, frowning. Timber eagerly nosed the dirt.

"No." His voice sounded strained.

Lily watched as Timber continued to sniff the ground, then put her nose up.

"I don't think we're alone here."

Lily looked up at Travis. His face was serious, with no hint of a smile. His body was tense, his shoulders slightly higher than a relaxed pose.

"Who else would be here?" she asked. The person after them? But no one had come down the trail after them, and Lily had even done her best to pay attention to see if any cars had followed them to the lot. She was sure that Travis would have done the same. So if there was someone else here, they would have arrived before she and Travis did.

But who else knew the significance of this particular spot?

"I have no idea. Not very many people." Even the way he said it showed how doubtful he was also feeling about this situation.

She and Travis knew this was where he had hidden. Matt had known, obviously, but he was dead. Could the narcotics gang have somehow found out an officer had been hiding there that night? But even if they had, what could they want with the old hiding spot now?

"You don't think it's someone, you

know, from the police department," she asked. "Do you?"

Travis didn't meet her eyes. Finally he blew out a breath. "I just don't know."

He knelt beside Timber and started to push the piles of loose dirt around. As Lily watched, Travis shifted enough dirt aside to reveal a hole, about six by twelve inches.

"Something was there," he muttered, digging some more.

It looked to Lily like something out of a novel. The fully exposed cavity was rectangular, with fairly smooth sides. It hadn't been a rushed job to bury whatever had been here.

And now someone had to come to retrieve it.

"What, though?" she asked aloud, but Travis just shook his head.

Beside them, Timber whined, pawed at the ground and started to sniff again.

"You okay?" Lily frowned. She moved

to check the dog for old injuries like the vet had shown her shortly after APD had given Timber to her. Right now, she was clearly uncomfortable in some way, but Lily couldn't find any obvious signs of injury—no part of the dog flinched when Lily ran her hands over her. "I don't understand what's wrong with her."

Timber laid down. Whined again.

"She's alerting," Travis said. "Sort of. Nothing she's doing is following the playbook exactly. But she smells something, clearly."

"Do you know what?"

Travis frowned but didn't answer. Lily didn't know if he was avoiding her question or if he really didn't know.

Suddenly coming here didn't seem like such a great idea. She had somehow felt reasonably safe on this trail, even with the way it was such a dark part of her past. Apparently she wasn't safe.

Maybe she wasn't safe anywhere.

The urgency to find out who was behind this rose in Lily's mind. This was not a sustainable way to live.

Timber stood and continued to sniff and track something, Travis followed her.

Lily watched Travis. He was a natural in this situation, reading the dog's body movements. "You're really good with her," she said at last, hoping saying so wouldn't interrupt him.

"I used to work with her all the time."

"Wait, you did?" Had Lily known that? She'd thought only Matt handled Timber.

"Yep."

Had she made that assumption because Timber had gone to her when she retired? As far as she understood, protocol usually dictated that a retired dog would go to a handler to be a pet. "Then why do I have her? I mean, did you not want her after..."

Travis looked in her direction. "I didn't want you to be alone."

Oh.

He'd given up Timber for her? She didn't know what to say to that or how to convey her thanks, but she appreciated it.

She had more questions but knew now wasn't the time. For one thing, was he planning to go back to police work? The way he paid attention to every detail, his eyes easily moving across the landscape, spoke to how good he had been at his job. Lily couldn't imagine him doing anything else, really. He seemed like he was made for it.

She stood still, looking around now and then to make sure there was no obvious threat nearby. She saw nothing, but then would she if there truly was anyone waiting for them out here? So far she'd been taken off guard every single time. It was distressing but true.

Finally, Travis walked back to where Lily was standing. "Something's wrong here. I think we should go."

Lily nodded. Her eyes went to the mudflats in front of them, just a bit farther down the hill, and out to the water. For what had to be the thousandth time, she imagined what it had been like for Matt.

How the events of his death could have anything to do with her in a way that made someone target her, she had no idea. If someone connected to that case was after her…why? And why now, after a full year had passed? It didn't seem reasonable to her at all—they would have come after her immediately if she was a target because of the case, she was almost sure of it.

But it was only her connection to Matt

that tied her to it at all. Lily couldn't make sense of it.

She and Travis hurried back up the hill, not talking, but as he walked her to her car, she finally told him all she'd been thinking.

"You're right that someone trying to hurt you because of Matt seems strange," he agreed.

"Is it just related to me finding the body? Maybe that's the only part that involves me?"

"Your house was on fire as soon as you got down the mountain. How did your attacker know where you lived?"

That was something she hadn't considered. Lily frowned.

"Oh, unless it was because of the note? Maybe...yeah, I've got nothing."

"Stuck again there, too," Travis said. "Why was your address on a piece of paper to start with? If you aren't tied to the case at all, that makes no sense."

Lily hated this. Ending up in her own personal suspense story was not a life goal, and it was something she'd really like to change.

"I just don't know," she finally said. "But I've got to drive to my house. I'm planning to call a contractor on the way home and figure out what's going to be necessary to repair the damage in the study."

"Mind if I come over?"

"You don't trust me alone?"

"I trust you fine. Do I trust whoever is after you to leave you alone? Not at all."

Lily appreciated that he cared, but it rubbed a little that he felt like she needed constant supervision. "You're not over-reacting?"

"Did the gunshots last night not answer that question?"

Okay, so he had a point. But she was still moving back home. If she wasn't safe anywhere, she at least wanted to be somewhere familiar, around her own things, have some home field advantage. As nice as Travis's house was, it wasn't hers. She needed something of her own around her right now.

She tried to explain that to Travis, but either it was just a way that they were different or it was a man thing, She could tell that, much as she tried, he just didn't get it.

Calling Timber toward her, she opened the door of her car, let the dog jump in and then climbed in after, bracing herself for whatever she was going to find at home.

If anything had convinced him that there was something more sinister going on here than they were aware of, it was Timber's behavior today. Travis couldn't stop thinking about it as he drove toward Lily's house.

Nothing about how she'd reacted was

typical, and all of it concerned him. Her behavior along with what they'd found made him uncomfortable.

Someone with a connection to the police department had almost certainly been involved in the narcotics ring. And not in a way that involved investigating it. Someone had gone bad.

He hated bad cops, hated storylines with bad cops. He rejected the narrative that law enforcement was somehow more likely to "go bad" than other professions. But none of his personal preferences or feelings made what they were dealing with now any less true. Someone had gone to the other side.

As he pulled into Lily's driveway, he breathed a sigh of relief to see that everything looked normal. Her car was parked neatly and not like she'd been in a hurry. He didn't see signs of anyone else being there. Nothing was on fire.

He walked to the front door and

knocked, feeling like he'd gone back in time. The idea of knocking on the door where she lived was as familiar to him as his own face.

She opened the door after only a few seconds. "You're here."

"Everything okay?"

"Yeah, it's just creepier than I antic-ipated." She shuddered, then looked down at the dog who was faithfully by her side. "If it weren't for Timber, it would be so much worse. At least I have her. Thank you for that, by the way."

She smiled at him, and he'd have given her the dog over and over to see that smile. He nodded. "So how does the study look? What's the damage like?"

She led him through the house, which he admired as they walked, to the back corner of the house. It was the most iso-lated spot of the house, he noticed. Was that why it had been the target? Just be-cause it was least likely to be caught in time? Or had there been a specific reason to start the fire in that room?

"What did the fire department say?" he asked.

"The structure is safe, if that's what you're wondering."

"No, I mean the cause of the fire. Do they know what it was yet?"

Lily nodded. "I called them back when I got here and realized they hadn't actually told me that. It was human caused. Arson."

Arson. Had the person responsible expected Lily to be home? Attempted murder? Or had it been meant as a warning?

As they entered the study, Travis tried to notice the details of his surroundings. This was a nice room, very much the kind of study he'd have imagined for Lily. The bookshelves were made of a warm medium-toned wood, packed with books. None of that appeared to be damaged, which he imagined was a relief to her. The ceiling was charred, and the logs on the outer wall had sustained smoke damage. It appeared to all be cosmetic, they'd caught it in time, but it wasn't pretty.

"Nothing is too bad besides that wall."

"I noticed that, too." Lily sighed. "I put that in. Well, me and Matt."

"Yeah?" He didn't love thinking about her with another man, but he was still curious about the details of her life and besides, he couldn't guarantee that didn't have something to do with the case.

"Yeah, I really wanted some traditional kinds of details in here and fell in love with these log accent walls. They're hollow, so they're not as heavy as regular logs. They're wood but not entirely natural, I think? I don't know, Matt found them online, and I loved them."

"Did he spend a lot of time here?"

"He didn't live here, if that's what you're asking me not so subtly. Honestly,

Travis, just because I started to think maybe God didn't care about every single detail doesn't mean I abandoned absolutely everything I was taught."

Her exasperated look couldn't dim the relief he felt at hearing that. It wouldn't have changed his feelings for her, but he'd hated to consider that she and Matt may have lived together. Lily deserved to be treated better than that, for one thing. For another, she was right, they had been taught differently.

"He wanted to," she finally admitted. "But I wasn't comfortable taking things that far, in any capacity. But he did hang out here a good bit, and like I said, we spent some time renovating this room, putting a backsplash in the kitchen, just general stuff like that to make it look better. Personalize it a bit."

"You must really like the house."

Lily shrugged. "I do. But I could move. It's been a good house, but it's pretty isolated. I'm seeing how that can be a bad thing."

Her lack of neighbors was somewhat concerning. Set on the side of a mountain, it was a fantastic retreat for solitude. But there was no one really close enough to know if Lily needed help, which was part of Travis's hesitation about leaving her alone.

"Do you have someone in mind to do the work for you?" he asked.

"Yeah, I called a contractor already, someone Hannah from work used in the past. He's supposed to come tomorrow."

Travis nodded. "Good."

The conversation lulled. Travis's mind was packed full of details about the case, Timber's strange behavior, his realization someone he knew personally had to be involved… So many questions.

"So…do you need to go right away?" she asked. "Or we could try to sort more things out? I'm assuming you have that case file of Matt's somewhere? I feel like you've rarely been without it."

Her voice was teasing, but he could tell that the heaviness of the day and the entire situation was starting to weigh on her as well.

"I can stay for a while." He didn't have any other plans for the night. His only current issue was not wanting to leave her alone, but he'd called the police department to confirm that they'd be upping patrols in the area for the time being. That was going to have to be good enough.

"We could eat first? I've got frozen pizza. I know that's not quite the same as the home-cooked meals you keep feeding me."

"It's good enough."

They headed into the kitchen, as Travis wrestled with how much he should tell her. He only had suspicions. Part of him didn't want to pass those on to her when they left him feeling so discouraged. But if it were him, he'd want to know absolutely everything he could about the situation.

As Lily preheated the oven, he decided it was better to tell her some of his thoughts, even though they were incomplete, than not.

"I'm convinced at this point that someone from the police department was involved." There was no cushioning the words. He felt the impact they had on her.

"What?" She shook her head as though clearing her mind. "I heard you. And I've heard you mention it as a possibility but I dismissed it I guess. I just can't... So you think someone who knew Matt—" she frowned "—set him up?"

He hadn't gotten that far into the tangle of this yet, but yeah, that was all that made sense.

"I want to find whoever this is. Really

badly." Lily's face darkened. Abruptly, she reached into the pantry and handed him two paper plates from a stack. "Set these on the table for me?"

Once the pizza came out of the oven, they were quiet for a while as they sat down and started to eat.

"Maybe we should make a list of all the names who were even sort of connected to Matt's death," Lily said at last. "Ignore motive for now since there's not a single motive involving me that makes sense."

Travis nodded. It was a good idea and something he'd already planned to do tonight. "I think we should."

Once dinner was finished, they headed into the living room. She pulled out a piece of paper, took a deep breath and handed it to Travis.

More than anything since Matt's death, this was going to hurt. He didn't want to consider that someone he knew could be capable of murder, but he didn't see any other explanation.

"Ready?" he asked Lily, and she nodded.

He picked up his pen and started to write.

THIRTEEN

"I guess Officer Knox should be on there." Travis said aloud as he wrote the name down. "Though, frankly, I can't see it."

Lily didn't think that meant much of anything. It was awful to contemplate anyone doing what the person behind all this had done, much less someone Travis was acquainted with. "Can you imagine anyone you know being involved?"

"No." He shook his head. "Definitely not."

"So just write the names. Everyone connected to the case. Who else?"

"Me. Matt."

Lily made a face. "I think we can safely rule the two of you out."

"I'm just writing anyone with any connection at all. We qualify." He wrote those names and then looked back up at her, as though waiting for her agreement.

"I mean, I guess."

He wrote for another minute or two, adding names aloud, but none of them meant anything to her.

"More people from the police department?" she asked.

"Mostly. A couple search-and-rescue workers, though that seems far-fetched with Timber behaving in such a strange way at the inlet today. It seems more likely it's someone who was directly involved with the investigation."

"How do you think she was reacting?" Lily asked. "I mean, I could tell she was acting strange, but what are your thoughts on it?"

"For one thing, I think she was confused. I don't know what about, but a lot of her behavior reads to me as confusion. Her mixed signals, alerting but only partially or incorrectly... Something isn't making sense to her about all this."

Lily reached down to pet her. "I get that, girl." She looked up at Travis. "Okay, what else?"

"She acted like she *wanted* to alert to something. Whatever scent she was catching, she seemed really interested in it."

"Should we take her back there?" Lily was still petting her, but Timber hadn't looked up. She seemed exhausted.

"I don't think so. Not anytime soon, anyway. She's too shaken up."

Travis fell silent then, and much as Lily had hoped they could brainstorm more, she felt like maybe she'd hit a wall for tonight. "Want to give it up for now?" she asked him.

"And do what instead?"

She shrugged. "You can head home if you want. I'm probably okay here." She did her best to ignore the fluttering in her stomach. Overactive nerves, nothing she needed to pay attention to.

"I'd rather stick around a bit longer, if that's okay."

"Watch a movie?" she offered, reaching for the remote control. They'd loved watching movies together back in the day, especially old John Wayne movies no one else had ever heard of.

The grin on his face warmed her inside. "Sounds good."

As they set up the movie and started to watch, Lily felt her shoulders relax for the first time all day. She was back home. The damage from the fire was bad, but not something she couldn't handle. She had a friend…

Her eyes went to Travis.

She'd insisted earlier that was all they could be, friends, and Travis hadn't argued with her. But Lily was second-guessing herself now. Sure, she still had many things left on her list to accomplish, but did she really want to risk losing him from her life again?

As they watched the movie, the thoughts danced in her mind, twisted and tangled. Maybe that was why almost without thinking, she reached over and took his hand.

The touch of his skin against hers startled her even though she was the one who had initiated it. It was as though being connected even in such a small way, holding his hand, was reminding her how much she cared about him. How much she loved…

How much she loved him?

She'd loved him once, she tried to tell

herself, but that didn't mean she loved him now.

Even though he came the second she'd called him. Even though he didn't push her at all and put others above himself and always had, the entire time she'd known him.

Lily's heart beat faster, and she found herself paying less and less attention to the movie and more to Travis's hand. He'd shifted so it was enveloping hers. He was so solid and dependable, but if those were the only qualities she cared about, she had Timber, too. But he was giving and intentionally put her above himself.

Her reasons for breaking up with him seemed thinner and thinner.

"Travis…" She looked up from his hand—their hands—to meet his eyes. She tried to figure out what he was thinking. Should she wait for some kind of clearer indications of his feelings?

But it hardly felt like a time for playing it safe, with danger surrounding them. This one moment of quiet in the midst of it all might be their only chance to be like this.

Lily didn't break eye contact. At the moment she was fully aware of the fact that she'd been the one to break the kiss the last time, she'd been the one to apologize for it, and yet she was the one who was seriously contemplating a repeat.

When she moved toward him, he didn't back up. Slowly, she let her eyes go to his lips, then looked back up at him. "Remember how we used to just sit and talk?"

He laughed softly. "Yeah, we talked for hours."

"I miss that."

This time, Lily was pretty sure he was the one who moved closer.

"You know how I said earlier we should

be just friends?" she asked. "I don't know anymore."

"What do you mean?"

"I mean... I think I want to kiss you."

She moved her lips within a breath of his, swallowed hard and waited.

He didn't move.

Lily kissed him gently. Fully. Slowly.

When he pulled away, she started talking. "What do you think, Travis? I know I said let's be friends, but... I mean, do you think you could even forgive me for...everything?"

"I forgave you years ago," he said, his voice barely louder than a whisper. Lily closed the distance between them even more. Their noses were almost touching. "But..."

Something was holding him back. She'd been able to tell even in the kiss. For once, she felt like she might be ready to really take a risk. She'd thought her list was risky, brave, adventurous. But maybe sometimes just living normal life was the real adventure.

"What is it?" she asked, half afraid to breathe as she waited for his answer.

"You didn't want this. Friends, remember?"

She looked away for half a second, then looked back at him. "What if I've changed my mind?"

She waited for his answer for what seemed like minutes.

"I just…" He moved away from her and stood up. "Let me think, Lily. I don't want to hurt you. I don't want anyone to get hurt."

"But I won't… I'm not…"

"It's late. Can we talk about it tomorrow?"

She felt her eyes sting, but she blinked the tears away and nodded. He wasn't asking for anything unreasonable. The logical side of her knew he was right, it was late. It was understandable that he didn't want to say anything or commit to anything that he might regret in the future.

So why did it still feel suspiciously like rejection?

"Sure." Lily stood, too, and walked toward the door to see him out. "No problem. I'll, uh, see you tomorrow after work?"

"Sounds like a plan. I'll work on figuring out how we can best spend our time and what we need to focus on."

Lily nodded along with him, barely hearing what he said, desperate for the night to end so they could just start over on less awkward footing tomorrow.

He told her good night and walked outside, and she locked the door behind him.

Lily knew that he hadn't said anything definite, but she was pretty sure she knew his answer. She'd had her chance.

And Travis wasn't taking another one on a relationship with her again.

Nothing was going to help him sleep tonight.

First, Travis had paced the floor of his house, suddenly understanding why fictional characters in movies liked to pace so much. There was something about it that made him feel slightly better, but it didn't come close to untangling his mind.

The case had to remain his top focus. He was worried that he was going to get Lily hurt, or worse, if he let himself be distracted by anything and that included a relationship with her. At the same time, he knew that her admission tonight had cost her. Her eyes had shone with something—he didn't dare call it love, that seemed too optimistic—maybe vulnerability? Then they'd flickered with some kind of hurt when he left without much explanation. But he hadn't wanted to get any more carried away by the trip down memory lane.

He liked her. More than liked her, he loved her. He had for years, and that wasn't going to change now.

He just wasn't sure about the timing. More than he wanted to see the two of them back together, he wanted them safe. His responsibility was to keep her safe more than anything else.

He walked into his kitchen and went through the motions of making himself a cup of coffee. He had just poured it when he heard a noise in the yard. He crept to the window and looked outside into the dimness. It wasn't yet dark enough to take away visibility. Was that…someone near his cabin? Creeping around in the dark?

There was no other explanation. He started to the door, then stopped, realizing he didn't have any kind of weapon on him. Tracking the intruder without one would be foolish and dangerous. He hurried to his bedroom, opened his gun safe and pulled out his handgun. He grabbed a gun belt with a holster already on it and fastened it quickly.

He opened the door slowly, making almost no noise. But getting the gun had taken some time, and he didn't have a visual on the intruder anymore.

The temperature had dropped since he'd gotten home. He shivered in the nighttime chill as he moved softly in the direction of the guest cabin.

Did whoever it was know that Lily wasn't there anymore? Or had her attacker come back to try to finish what he'd started the other day?

Even though Lily should be safely in her own house, dread sank into the pit of his stomach anyway. The situation was truly desperate, the threat against Lily terribly real. It frustrated him that no matter how hard he tried to get away from the sometimes oppressive lack of hope in police work—the uncertainty, anxiety and reminders of the darkness in the world—he'd been pulled back in.

Was ignoring it the answer? Should he continue working with his brother? Or was it time to go back?

Strange that this was the second time that question had crossed his mind in as many days. He didn't quite know what to do with that. Even if he was supposed to go back, he'd have preferred to figure it out in some way other than Lily facing danger. He didn't want her hurt, and he was terrified that he was going to mess up.

Right now, though, she wasn't here. And the situation in front of him had to be dealt with. One hand on his weapon, he moved toward the front door of the empty cabin.

Walking into the darkened cabin felt

like going back in time several years, but he took only a second or two to let his eyes adjust before he kept moving forward. Standing still could be deadly in situations like this; hesitation could kill.

Although, so could crashing into something you weren't entirely prepared for.

His ears registered the sound of movement just as something slammed into his shoulders, missing his head only by inches. Desperately trying to remember everything he'd ever learned about hand-to-hand combat, he fought back.

The man was strong, Travis noticed immediately. He'd thought when the man bested him last time that it was just because he hadn't been paying enough attention, but he was just flat-out outmuscled.

But he wasn't giving up. He punched and blocked to the best of his ability.

Then, as quickly as the man had appeared, he turned tail and ran.

Travis blinked for half a second. Why had he sprinted away in the middle of the fight? He sprinted after the man, but when he reached the front yard, he was gone. Again.

Travis kicked the ground. He moved slowly around the cabin, his eyes open, guard up. No sign of the attacker. The ground didn't yield anything trackable.

Why had he come here? To target Lily? Had he just not noticed she wasn't here? Travis was surprised. It had seemed like whoever was after her was better at tracking her movements than that.

Or had the man been looking for something? But what could it be? Even Lily seemed not to know why she was in this situation, so figuring out what she may or may not have would be difficult.

Catching his breath and doing his best to bring his heart rate back to a normal level, Travis walked back to his house. The night had grown even darker, but his senses were sharp and ready to spot trouble at the first sign. However, all was quiet as he headed back into the house and locked the door behind him.

He'd been in such a hurry earlier that he hadn't locked his own door. While he doubted that the man was waiting for him when he'd been in such a hurry to get away, Travis planned to be careful. Methodically, he cleared every room in the house.

Nothing. No sign of any intruder.

Travis went back to his coffee on the counter. Cold. Which made sense. He dumped it out, made himself another cup, then walked to his bedroom, set the coffee on the bedside table and eyed the bed. He couldn't see himself sleeping anytime soon. Instead, he moved to the chair in the corner and sat, sipping at his coffee.

Should he call Lily?

What was the point? She knew someone was after her. What had happened here tonight didn't directly affect her at this moment, he didn't think. Besides, Travis couldn't imagine that she was having any more luck getting to sleep and hated to be the reason she lost any more.

He took a deep breath and tried to relax. It was over, at least for tonight. The chances of anything else happening were slim. Their attacker would need to regroup, replan.

He took another sip of coffee, felt himself start to nod off and didn't try to keep himself awake.

FOURTEEN

The stillness of the night was too quiet for Lily to have any sort of peace. Maybe it was the chemistry between her and Travis earlier, then his subsequent semi-rejection and her mind's confusion about that whole situation. Or maybe it was because, much as she tried to put on a brave face, the idea of staying somewhere entirely alone when someone still wanted her dead was overwhelming and scary.

Should she have gone back to Travis's guest cabin? It was probably too late for that now. Maybe not? She could call him, and he'd probably answer. He always did, didn't he?

All the more reason she should tough it out, at least for tonight. She'd inconvenienced him enough.

Lily turned over on her pillow and opened her eyes. Outside it was dark, so it had to be around two in the morning. There weren't many hours this time of year when the world was fully dark outside.

She could do this. She could fall asleep and wake up in a few hours and sort out all the things going on in her life that weren't going well.

Something inside her whispered that it would be easier if she let God help her work things out, but she resisted it. She didn't need God like that anymore, did she? Matt had been sure she didn't.

Then again, Matt wasn't here.

Travis was just as independent, proud and capable as Matt, if not more—though thinking that felt slightly disloyal. Yet he believed that he needed God every day, all the time.

It was more than Lily could sort out right now.

She closed her eyes and willed herself to sleep.

When she opened her eyes again, the world outside was slightly lighter with hints of dawn creeping across the Alaskan sky. Lily relaxed and blew out a breath. Today she'd talk to Travis and tell him she was willing to look into other accommodations. It didn't have to be his guest cabin, but being alone seemed like a terrible idea. Last night wasn't one she wanted to experience again.

Strongly, she felt colder than she had earlier. Lily patted the bed beside her, where Timber always slept. Nothing.

Where was Timber?

Doing her best not to panic, Lily sat

straight up in bed and blinked until it felt like sleep had absolutely no hold on her. She swung her legs over the side of the bed and slid into her slippers, partially for warmth and partially to muffle the noise of her movement. She grabbed her phone from the bedside table, though she didn't text Travis. She was tired of bothering him. Timber had probably wandered off to get some water, or maybe patrol the house.

Although it was unusual for her to do either. Typically Timber came to bed with her, got up maybe once right at the start of the night to do a lap around the house, then slept soundly. Lily didn't know what to think about the dog not being there when she woke, but it didn't seem good.

Heart pounding, Lily waited for her eyes to adjust to the nearly dark room— some light was making its way in through the window now but the sky outside was still a dark early morning blue. Not nearly enough light to actually see by. But enough to know for sure that Timber wasn't anywhere in this room. Lily felt her breathing quickening even as she tried to find more logical reasons for Timber to be gone than the one that haunted her brain.

What if someone was in the house? What if Timber had gone after them?

What if something had happened to Timber?

The what-ifs tormented her as she walked into her bathroom. No Timber there, either. Taking a deep breath, she moved toward the bedroom door, then hesitated. She pulled out her phone and sent a quick text to Travis.

Sorry to wake you. Something weird is going on, I can't find Timber. Maybe it's fine? I feel silly texting.

Lily hesitated before pressing Send, but finally hit it. Maybe he wouldn't notice. Or maybe he'd come right over, which was something she wanted more than she was willing to admit. She moved to the door of her bedroom and eased it open.

Walking out in the main area of the house took more courage than anything Lily had attempted in a while. The living room had fewer windows than her room, and she could barely see. After a minute of struggling against the darkness, she stopped. She would do what she'd seen Timber do many times and just listen. Maybe she'd hear something she wouldn't otherwise.

Freezing in place, Lily waited. Her ears didn't tell her anything, though. There was just silence.

Which actually did tell her something. Something was wrong with Timber.

Lily's imagination sped up, running

over all the awful situations the dog could have found herself in. Surely someone wouldn't have…

It took every ounce of self-restraint she had not to yell out Timber's name as panic rose within her. Lily was wide awake now, and she moved through the living room, doing her best to scan every piece of furniture, every inch of floor.

She shivered, anxiety chilling her, then stopped in the middle of the room. She looked to the left, toward the front door.

It was standing wide open. And on the floor in front of the door was Timber, lying still in the moonlight.

Lily almost screamed, so great was her horror, but she knew if anyone was still in the house it would alert them to her location.

Rather than search the other rooms, she hurried to Timber's side, placed a hand on her soft fur and waited. Seconds passed. Then—

Up. Down. Up. Down.

She was breathing. She was alive.

Relief wrestled with panic as Lily worked to shove her hands under the dog's heavy body. She pulled Timber close to her chest and moved toward the bedroom, pulling the door shut behind her, latching it and locking it as quietly as she could.

Her heart was still pounding. Someone was in her house. Someone had hurt her dog.

She called 911, explained the situation to them, then called Travis, who didn't answer. She left a voicemail, trying to stay calm.

And then Lily sat on the bed beside her dog and waited.

As she sat, the urge to pray seemed to well up inside her until she couldn't ignore it anymore.

Had she prayed at any time lately? Or had it been years? She couldn't even remember anymore. All she knew was that more than anything right now, she wanted to know that Travis was right, that God really would show up and help.

I feel like I might have messed up. I don't know, God, who is right and who isn't between Travis and Matt, but if Travis is right, and You do actually care, please save my dog. I don't deserve it or anything, but I don't want her to die. I want her to be safe and me, too.

She squeezed her eyes shut to stop the tears that were threatening to come. Somehow she knew, though she hadn't been sure only minutes before, that God had heard her. Travis was right. She thought. Wasn't he?

As she sat on the bed, petting Timber and waiting, she kept praying, kept listening. She didn't hear anything.

But someone had clearly been in her house.

Why? They'd poisoned Timber, most likely. She was no investigator, but it seemed pretty obvious that Timber had been incapacitated somehow. But she'd have expected that whoever it was would come after her, take advantage of the fact that she was sleeping and kill her.

But they hadn't. Why?

A soft knock at her bedroom door startled her enough that she jumped. Then Lily felt for Timber's ribs again, confirmed that she was breathing and walked to the door. Her hand was on the knob, about to unlock it, when she froze.

Was this Travis coming to help? Or had the intruder come to finish the job?

Speaking of breaking in, how had the door been opened? She hadn't noticed any damage, but she hadn't investigated closely because she was focused on Timber.

Deciding that the risk was worth it, she eased the door open and met Travis's eyes through the crack in the door.

Something inside her broke.

But in a good way, like it needed to be broken.

Tears streamed down her face for the first time that night, and Lily cried, something in her feeling like she finally could. As though because Travis was here, she didn't have to be strong for Timber anymore.

If Timber even knew she was here. The dog seemed entirely unconscious.

"I'm so glad you're here," she said, wiping a tear from her face that somehow didn't embarrass her. Matt had made her feel bad for her tears, for any kind of large show of emotion really, but with Travis she could just be herself. She could feel how she felt.

"What's wrong?" Travis asked in a rush. "What happened?"

"Didn't you see the door?"

"What about it?"

"It was wide open, someone… I guess someone was in the house?"

Travis hesitated. "It was closed. The door was closed."

Lily blinked. She was sure she hadn't imagined the door being open. She'd seen Timber on the floor in the moonlight. And Timber was unconscious on the bed right now, which proved that she hadn't made it all up.

"I believe you, I mean," Travis clarified quickly, which she appreciated. "But it was shut."

"So either someone left or wants us to think they did."

"One of those probably. Strange." He frowned. "And Timber? What's wrong? Wait, she's not…"

His voice trailed off, and Lily reached for his hand without thinking. She squeezed it quickly before letting it drop.

"She's alive. But I don't know what's wrong."

Travis walked over and examined Timber, opening her mouth and looking at her gums. He turned back to Lily. "I think she's going to be okay. She seems drugged? Honestly she seems like she's been given a sedative. This is exactly how they described it in one of the trainings we had."

Lily nodded, though her face pinched into a frown. "How long until she wakes up? Should we take her to the vet?"

It was so easy to include him in her decision-making processes. It felt right.

"I think she'll be okay. Let's give it a little time." He ran his hand along the length of Timber's body, then looked up at Lily. "Someone probably drugged her so they could get in without worrying about her."

It gave more weight to their idea that

Sarah Varland 289

it was some type of first responder involved in Matt's case.

Lily felt a heaviness settle over her.
Even though they had no other leads,
it felt wrong that someone who had
worked with Matt could be trying to
kill her now.

They had to solve this. For her own
peace of mind, they had to.

Lily didn't look like she'd slept. Of
course, he could hardly blame her. The
amount of stress they were both under,
with the case and trying to figure out…
well, whatever they were trying to figure out about the two of them.

Timber had started to stir not long
after he'd told Lily his suspicions about
her having been sedated. They offered
her some water, which she accepted
gratefully. Still, he thought it was a better idea that she rest. So Timber was
locked in Lily's bedroom while he and

Lily took a look around the house to see what had been disturbed.

He should have let Lily know about the intruder breaking into his house. Clearly he'd been bent on finding something, whether it was Lily or something he thought she had.

"Do you have any idea of anything he could be after?" Travis asked her. "Some kind of object, or evidence from the case…"

"You said it was a narcotics case, right?" She turned to him with raised eyebrows. "Since I don't have any narcotics, I'm going to have to go with no on that one."

He smiled a little at her attempt at middle-of-the-night humor, but persisted, "Seriously, anything you can think of, no matter how weird it sounds. Anything related to the case, Matt, anything."

"You think Matt himself could be the reason I'm a target, not just the case?"

Travis truly didn't know. He was grasping at straws at this point, but there just wasn't time to waste doing anything else. Every moment that passed with them walking around in the dark like this was another moment with Lily in danger. That was unacceptable.

"I think anything you have that's related to Matt is worth investigating," Travis said at last.

It felt odd to talk about Matt, especially Lily's relationship with him, but it was possible that something between them had value to the narcotics gang. Wasn't it?

Nothing made sense.

Lily moved through the house, commenting on little things here and there. Matt had given her that bench, they bought it from someone in the area who made furniture out of Sitka spruce, did

292 *K-9 Alaskan Defense*

that count? Travis thought no, though it was a nice bench. But the chance that someone had broken into her house in the middle of the night to get it were slim.

The truth was that Lily shouldn't be a target. Her house was meticulously organized, there were no unkempt piles of paper anywhere that could hide useful documents and she didn't have any of Matt's personal belongings since they'd never been married, and he'd had his own house. Who knew what had become of those after his death.

Finally, they made their way into the study.

"I don't think Matt gave me anything in here. Except labor, I mean. Lots of labor."

"He put the logs up, you said?" Travis nodded to the accent wall with its heavy fire damage.

"Yes," she affirmed. "And built in the

bookshelves. We spent the most time in here, probably. I'd read a book, and he'd work."

"Work?" Travis frowned. Most police work, even paperwork, was done at the department itself. It wasn't something that got taken home.

"Like I said, that undercover case seemed to keep him pretty busy."

Something still felt odd about that, but Travis wasn't sure if it was just the fact that undercover cases always left something of a bad taste. Deception never felt good, even when it was for a good cause.

Or maybe there was a reason that thought made him uncomfortable. How busy could Matt have been really? But with the doubt, there was once again the uncomfortable feeling that he shouldn't go looking too deeply into a dead man's secrets. Especially when he was falling for his ex-fiancée. It felt petty.

"This room." Lily stopped. "Something is weird in here."

They searched all over. Books out of place? No, Lily said. Any furniture moved? No.

Travis saw no help for it. "Let's get Timber. If she's better, I'll have her sniff around."

Easing the door to Lily's room open, Travis tried to be quiet in case Timber was sleeping off the drugs still. If she was, he didn't want to wake her. But when he stepped inside, she wasted no time jumping up on him. She looked much better, her eyes sharp.

"You're okay, aren't you?" he asked as he petted her.

Her eyes seemed to answer *yes*.

Travis turned to Lily. "Let's bring her out and see what she notices in the house. We won't go right to the study. It could be that there's something in another room we missed, but I also don't want to bias her against a particular room."

Lily nodded and opened the bedroom door.

Travis turned to Timber. "Timber, search."

The command included anything out of the ordinary and could turn up anything from a person to hidden drugs in a normal police investigation. Travis wasn't expecting to find either of those, but it would be interesting to see what she would come up with.

Timber ran first to the front door and whined.

"That's where I found her," Lily said, anguish clear on her face. That had to have been hard.

Travis put a hand on her upper arm, and she smiled at him. Maybe everything wasn't messed up after last night. Maybe they could figure this out after all.

Timber moved around the living room,

clearly on alert but not keying in on anything. The same went for the kitchen. And the guest bathroom.

She ran to the study last. Stopped in the doorway. And whined.

The noise immediately made Travis's chest tighten with anxiety. She sounded exactly as she had the day before at the inlet where she'd seemed confused.

Even Lily seemed to notice. A frown stretched across her face, and she glanced over at Travis. "Is she doing it again?"

Timber moved into the room and sniffed with her nose in the air. She whined and looked back at Travis. It wasn't quite an alert, but it was something. More than just *something*. It was concerning and unnerving.

What smell was upsetting her so much? Why was she acting like she didn't know what she was supposed to be doing?

Her retirement had purely been for physical reasons. She'd been shot the night Matt had died and hadn't been able to go back into the field as a police K-9 because of that. Otherwise, she was fine. Her abilities, her intelligence, all of that remained unchanged.

So what was with her odd reaction?

Nothing about this felt right. And it felt entirely too much like her behavior earlier by the inlet to be coincidence.

But what did these two places have in common?

FIFTEEN

Lily stood in her study and watched her dog and Travis, waiting for him to explain to her what all of this meant.

"Something isn't right," Travis said at last.

That much was clear to her already. Lily threw him a look, hoping that thought was communicated.

Her cell phone rang.

"Hello?" She stepped out of the room, since Timber's whining was loud enough to be distracted on a phone call.

"Lily Peterson?"

"Yes."

"This is Officer Keller. Could you come down to the Silvertip Creek Police Department? We need to talk about some of what we found."

Lily glanced back into the study, at Timber who was still out of sorts. Was Travis right that the drugs hadn't affected her? Or should she be seen by a vet?

"Uh…" She glanced at her watch. "Okay, I'll come down. It might be a little while? You know it's only 5:00 a.m.?"

Officer Keller laughed. "Sorry. I couldn't sleep. Came in early and had news waiting." Her voice sobered. "You definitely need to come in as soon as possible."

"Okay. I'll be there soon." Lily hung up, frowning at the phone. That call made about as much sense as Timber's behavior.

She relayed the news to Travis.

"We'd better get down there then," Travis said. "That's really unusual."

Was there anything about this case that wasn't?

They called Timber out of the study and shut the door. That seemed to help, though she still seemed a little anxious even in the rest of the house.

"If I had to guess, I'd say whatever smell it is that's causing her to react that way is concentrated in the study," Travis said. "But there's enough of it in the rest of the house to make her somewhat upset."

"I guess I could see that, but what is it? Drugs?" Lily asked. It was the only thing that made even little bit of sense.

He was shaking his head. He didn't know.

She could feel his frustration and wished she could reassure him that everything was okay, but the fact was it wasn't. They both needed answers, and nothing about their situation was okay.

"Maybe whatever the police found out

will help," she muttered and moved toward her bedroom. "I'm going to get dressed. I'll meet you back out here? That is, if you want to go together to the police department. I didn't mean to assume."

Travis reached out and squeezed her hand.

Lily looked down at where their hands were touching, then back up at him.

"I'm going with you," he said. He dropped her hand to motion quickly toward her bedroom. "Hurry. A phone call at five in the morning? I'm half afraid of whatever they're going to tell us."

"But it's good, right? Progress?"

"It's good," he confirmed. "Almost certainly. Any information is helpful. But I'm concerned that this early in the morning and wanting to tell you in person, whatever they've got is going to be earth-shattering."

Feeling anxious, Lily closed her bedroom door and started pulling out pieces to wear today—jeans, a long-sleeved T-shirt, a vest. The forecast called for rain today, which always cooled the temperature way down. It was amazing how cold fifty-five degrees without sunshine could be.

She hoped that whatever Travis was worried about didn't happen. He was reminding her a little of Timber right now. He seemed upset, but she didn't know if he could exactly articulate why.

Still, she was excited about whatever they might find out. Whatever it was, it had to be better than not knowing.

The drive to the police department was somewhat quiet. Lily looked out the window. Travis wondered what she was thinking about. His own stomach was churning as he drove.

"Mind if we make a quick stop?" Lily asked.

Travis shook his head. "That's fine, where to?"

"Swing into my coffee shop, if you would. I desperately need a cup of coffee and one of Hannah's cinnamon rolls."

He turned into the shop's parking lot. The Open sign was off, as he'd expected, but the lights inside were still out. "I have bad news, but I don't think your shop's open. Maybe the owner had a crazy night and isn't at work yet."

She laughed at his completely awful joke. "Maybe. But Hannah's here baking already in the back. Come on." She climbed out of the car and motioned for him to follow. Timber trotted along beside her.

They walked up to the front door, and Travis watched as Lily pulled out a key. She eased it into the door and motioned for him to go in before her. She followed, and he glanced back to make sure she locked the door behind them.

"You sure about this?" he asked. "I don't mind buying somewhere."

Lily laughed. "Seriously, what good is owning a coffee shop if I can't go in and get coffee on what has so far been a rough morning?"

He couldn't fight her there.

Lily walked confidently through the front of the shop, flipping on a small lamp. The massive glass windows in the front were a security risk, he realized. If this dragged on for much longer, he'd want to talk to her about making her workplace less vulnerable. Or maybe talk her into taking some time off work.

Though he could imagine what the response to that would be.

"Morning, Hannah," Lily said as she walked into the kitchen. Sure enough, a woman was already back there baking.

"Good morning." Hannah barely looked up. "Cinnamon roll?"

"Please. Two."

Travis was only too happy to take the cinnamon roll that Lily offered him, and the coffee she'd made like it was nothing. "You're really good at this." She laughed off his compliment as they walked back to the car, so he tried again. "No, really. You're very good at this. You were onto something with that list."

Lily's face fell instantly, and he opened his mouth to backtrack, but she held a hand up and cut him off. "I really still feel bad. I don't think…"

He shook his head. "You had dreams, I get it. You don't have to keep apologizing."

She stopped in the parking lot, and he stopped beside her. "What if they cost me another dream?" she asked.

He didn't have to be a genius to know she was talking about them.

They were words he'd waited for years to hear, really, and hearing them hit him every bit as hard as he would have expected. But once again it was like something inside was slowing him down, telling him to wait.

He reached for her hand and squeezed it. "Let's deal with all this first."

He was ready for a happily-ever-after, but in his experience, nothing worth having came this easily.

They climbed back into the car, and Travis drove them to the police department where they parked and walked inside.

This building was much smaller than the Anchorage Police Department's impressive structure, very small town. But it was adequate for the level of crime that Silvertip Creek usually dealt with, which wasn't much.

The entry was well lit, almost friendly. Again, fitting for a town where the police were typically called on for things like search and rescue or neighborhood patrolling to discourage the occasional small crime.

A murder discovered on one of their mountain ridges wasn't typical for Silvertip Creek at all.

For half a second, Travis pictured himself working here and didn't hate the idea. Maybe police work wasn't something he had to be entirely done with after all? Just because he was done with the pace and tension of Anchorage didn't mean that he had to be done entirely, did it?

Officer Keller met them in the lobby, looking relieved. "Thanks for coming down," she said immediately, then seemed to eye Lily carefully. "We have something we need to talk about."

Lily nodded. "No problem."

Travis didn't like the way Officer Keller seemed so cautious around Lily. Again, the sense of foreboding he'd had earlier haunted the edges of his mind. What had the police discovered?

"We have results back from the note and key you found at the scene," Officer Keller said at last. "We found the fingerprints of several men on it. One is Arnold Harris, the man you found on the ridgeline."

Lily looked over at him, and Travis fill in the other blanks. "The man accused of killing Matt that night."

Officer Keller cleared her throat. "And... well, Matt."

"Matt Davis?" Travis clarified. "The police officer?" He glanced at Lily. "So Arnold had that note for..."

Officer Keller was already shaking her head. The uncomfortable pit in Travis's stomach deepened.

"We investigated the murder scene on Avalanche Peak carefully," she said. "We were able to find the murder weapon and run prints on it, too." Her gaze shifted between Lily and Travis and back again. And then she said the words that Travis had been dreading and yet somehow expecting ever since Timber began acting strangely at the inlet.

"The prints on the murder weapon— which was a knife—also belong to Matt Davis."

Silence had never felt so violently loud.

Travis didn't know whether to reach for Lily's hand or give her a minute. The expressions crossing her face told him the words were still sinking in. Being rejected. Denied.

"Wait, but Matt... He's dead," Lily said at last. "He was an officer, but he's..."

"He's not dead." Officer Keller didn't sugarcoat the words at all, and they fell on the room with the gentleness of an anvil. "And he is now wanted for the murder of Arnold Harris."

* * *

He is now wanted for the murder of Arnold Harris.

The words echoed in Lily's mind, which seemed empty of all else. Matt wasn't dead. Matt was alive. Matt was a killer.

Every terrifying moment she'd experienced over the last few days shifted and darkened with new perspective. The man in her house? Matt.

Shooting at her in the woods? Matt.

The man who'd created the gruesome scene she'd stumbled onto on the mountain ridge, who had tried to push her off the mountain, who had burned part of her house?

Matt?

A wave of nausea crashed into her, and she reached her arms out, feeling for a wall, Travis's arm, a chair, anything that could steady her. Although was there anything that could steady someone who had been caught so off guard?

Travis' arms were around her, bracing, gentle. But her panic went too deep.

"I need a minute," she was able to say at last. She looked up at Travis, whose face spoke of something very much like pity. Maybe it was just kindness.

She'd thought it was bad before, having people think of her as the woman who had lost her fiancé in the line of duty. Now that life, that identity, was nothing more than a lie.

Matt's lie, which she had bought.

Matt, a killer?

The news seemed too strange to be true. She'd seen him be harsh to others, though Matt was nice to her, but still, a killer? She'd never have agreed to marry someone she could think capable of that.

The memory of the bloodstained ground around Arnold's body on the mountain ridge made her chest feel tight.

"I don't understand," she gasped.

"We don't, either," Officer Keller spoke

up. "That's all we know. Usually this is the kind of thing we wouldn't release immediately to the public, but you both need to be aware as it changes how you act."

Both Travis and Lily looked at Timber.

"That's why she was acting so strange," Travis said.

"She smelled Matt." Lily shook her head. It was too much. She didn't even know what to think, what to feel. Her immediate instinct was to never trust her instincts again—hadn't she almost ended up married to a murderer?

Why had he wanted to marry her anyway? Surely he hadn't really loved her, not if he was willing to kill her now that...now that what? She was in his way somehow?

"Our working assumption is that Matt must have been involved in the narcotics case beyond his official duties," Officer Keller explained. "I've got a call in to Officer Knox at APD, but he's not in the office yet."

Well, it was 6:00 a.m. That seemed logical. How much longer would they have to wait? This changed everything, she was sure. Lily was not going to work today, that was clear. They had to be close. They knew who was after her now, and while the situation was even more dangerous, it had to put them closer to finding him and stopping him.

Didn't it?

But Officer Keller's next statement urged caution. "This could last days, weeks, longer. The man has been presumed dead for a year, and somehow gotten away with it. He knows how to hide."

Lily looked at Travis. "My house. The logs. What if he hid something there?"

It seemed plausible enough. Quickly, all three of them headed for the parking lot, where Officer Keller got in a squad car and followed Travis and Lily back to Lily's place.

Her house looked different to her now. It was as if the knowledge that a killer had helped her renovate it, had spent time there, robbed it of its peacefulness.

Taking deep breath, bracing herself even though technically nothing had changed, Lily walked through the front door.

At her feet, Timber whined slightly, and compassion for her flooded Lily. How was Timber supposed to reconcile the fact that she smelled an intruder with the fact that the smell belonged to her former handler? Lily reached down and petted Timber.

The German shepherd looked up at her appreciatively.

"You're such a good dog," Lily said with all her heart. One good thing had come out of Matt's deep deception—

Timber belonged to her now and couldn't be taken away.

"You said the K-9 alerted in the study?" Officer Keller asked Travis.

He nodded. "Yes. And Lily had mentioned that the log wall was installed by Matt. Chances are good he hid something there." He trailed off at the end. "Could it be whatever had been dug up at the inlet, where Timber started acting strangely?"

Lily's eyes widened as she realized exactly what Travis meant. "What if both men were after whatever was buried there? Otherwise why would Arnold and Matt both have been on that ridge?"

Officer Keller looked surprised, but Travis just looked impressed.

"Let's take a look at the logs first," Officer Keller suggested at last. "Let's see what we've got." She led the way into the study.

It hit harder emotionally to be in a

room that had once symbolized so much happiness between Lily and Matt. She glanced down at Timber; the dog was still clearly confused. How would she react around Matt if he did ever see them in person again? Would Timber actually attack someone she'd once worked with? Or would Lily no longer be able to count on her to help protect her? She wasn't sure.

Lily watched as Travis bent down and talked to Timber. She couldn't quite hear what he was saying, but he ran though several exercises with her, having her sit, spin, run under his legs, lie down. After a few minutes, she'd noticeably settled down.

"Now let's see what she can find," he said, and Timber started to sniff.

They watched, waiting for what she would discover.

SIXTEEN

"There. She's alerting."

Timber was pawing at one of the logs in the wall that had been damaged by the fire. It was a few logs up from the bottom on the right side of the wall, and looked exactly like all the others.

"What is she alerting on?" Lily asked.

Lily spoke as if she was in a sort of trance. It had to be surreal to learn that Matt was still alive and a criminal all in one instant.

"Not sure." Travis knocked against the log Timber was focused on. It sounded hollow, but Lily had said they all were. He frowned. If something was stored in it, wouldn't it sound less hollow? He knocked slowly, over and over, down the length of the log. Then finally came to a spot that sounded slightly different.

He could tell as he looked around at Lily and then Officer Keller that they'd all heard it.

"Do you mind if I cut it open?" he asked Lily. "I could be wrong…"

"This room has to be redone anyway because of the fire." Her face was tight, her eyes anxious. "Yes. Just cut it."

It took a few minutes to find the right tool for the job, but Travis emerged from Lily's small garage with a saw after a few minutes. Without fanfare, he started to saw into the log.

Slowly, sawdust piled up on the floor. Travis's arms started to burn with the effort, which was mildly embarrassing.

The wood finally cracked. He stopped sawing and wiped sweat from his forehead with the back of his arm.

"Keep going." Lily was staring at the log, fixated.

He understood. Whatever they were about to find might finally hold some answers, answers she'd wanted for over a year now, though she hadn't known exactly what questions to ask.

Travis knew when this was all over, it would hit him hard that a brother in arms had gone bad like that. He liked to pretend it never happened, that everyone who entered the profession was honorable and true, but people were people in every job. Always some bad apples.

This one just seemed a bit more rotten than usual.

As the wood cracked, Travis poked at it with his fingers, trying to pry the gap wider. If this was why Matt had been in Lily's study, it was no wonder he hadn't gotten whatever was in here out yet. It wasn't a quick job or a quiet one. Maybe that had been the purpose of the fire, to destroy this wall…

In that case, whatever Matt was after should be in a fireproof safe.

The wood splintered against his hand as he jammed it in with too much force. Still not enough room, and not enough leverage to snap it. Wincing, Travis pulled his hand back out. "Almost there." He continued to saw.

Finally, he shoved his hand into the gap, at first feeling nothing but empty space.

Lily and Officer Keller were both watching, neither speaking. He felt their anticipation, the hope that this wasn't just leading to dead ends and more questions.

His fingertips hit something cold. Hard. A metal box.

Just like he'd expected.

Reaching his arm even farther in, he managed to wrap his fingers around the box and pull it toward him. He dragged it to the opening, which wasn't nearly large enough.

"You don't have a sledgehammer, do you?" he asked Lily.

"What is it?" Officer Keller asked eagerly.

"A box."

She nodded. "I'm calling Officer Knox from Anchorage on his cell. He needs to be here."

Travis agreed, tugging his hand out of the wall. He turned his attention to enlarging the opening in the wood enough to get the box out. After a few minutes of wrestling, jamming and sawing, he tugged it out and set it on the floor.

It wasn't large, probably five by eleven inches, maybe slightly bigger. And it was locked.

"The key!" Lily said.

Officer Keller pulled a bag out of her

pocket. Travis raised his eyebrows and she shrugged. "I brought it just in case."

Wearing a pair of gloves, she slid it out of the bag and into the safe's lock. It opened without a fight, smooth and easy.

Inside were stacks of papers, folded in half so they'd fit. Newspaper clippings, handwritten sticky notes. Financial statements for Weatherby Enterprises, a company in Anchorage they'd suspected might have ties to the narcotics ring.

He scanned through the statements, finding several lines that would account for illegal activities. Other lines caught his eye also.

"Davis Consulting."

Lily met his eyes. "Matt? Do you… I guess you usually don't get paid by the gangs in undercover ops." She reached for the statement, and Travis handed it to her.

"Maybe." He shrugged. "But we put

the funds in a dummy account that the department can access, never in someone's actual personal account, and these—" he ruffled through the papers "—appear to be Matt's statements."

Scrawled on them in someone's rough handwriting were notes about Matt's guilt—lists, dates, *evidence* that Matt wasn't who they thought he was.

"Someone else wrote these," Travis said.

"Yeah. But he's dead now."

The voice behind them was one Travis hadn't heard in a year.

He used to think of the voice as confident, useful to have with you in tight situations. Matt had never seemed scared of anything, and his confidence had always been inspiring.

Now Travis just heard coldness.

"I'm going to need that," Matt went on calmly.

Timber whined.

Officer Keller pulled her weapon, but Matt pulled his faster. He shot her, hitting her arm. She cried out and fell to the ground.

Lily yanked off her vest and knelt down, immediately pressing it against Officer Keller's wound. She stuffed something into her pocket, too, though Travis wasn't sure what.

Wait, she had one of the papers from the safe! A small amount of relief flooded through him.

Travis's heart pounded as he reached for the sidearm he knew was no longer in his holster. He'd had to remove it before going inside the police department and left it in his car. He was completely unprepared.

They all were.

If Lily had thought she'd feel more pain when she saw Matt's face again, she'd been wrong. Surely there would be a variety of emotions to deal with later, but right now all she felt was disgust. Anger.

His voice was cold and hard, and his eyes barely flickered when she turned and met his gaze. Who even was this man whose appearance she recognized, but whose actions didn't line up with the man she thought she'd known?

"You're not getting any of this." She looked up at him from where she knelt next to Officer Keller, who was mostly unconscious. Lily tried to say the words with more firmness than she felt.

Inside, she was shaking. They didn't have a plan from here.

Travis had noticed that something had been taken from the scene near the inlet. And now there was evidence hidden here in her house. Why had Arnold and Matt been up on Avalanche Peak? Was something hidden there also?

Her gut said yes, though it was likely Matt had retrieved it by now.

What was their best option? She wanted to talk to Travis, but there was no time. It surprised her how much she cared about his input.

That had been another stark difference between the two men, she realized now, looking at Matt's cold eyes. Travis listened to her, talked to her, communicated with her. Matt had just told her what to do. She'd not fully seen the difference until now.

But neither man could help her now. Matt was against her. Travis was stuck in the situation with her.

Her eyes darted to Timber.

"Don't even think about trying to turn her against me. It's basically impossible. Besides—" he patted the gun he'd put back on his hip in a slow, threatening way "—I don't want to shoot her, but I will."

"You poisoned Timber," Lily said suddenly. Of course she knew the dog had been given something to knock her out, but it hit so much harder realizing that someone Timber trusted had done that to her.

"It's hardly poison." He rolled his eyes. "I could have hurt her if I wanted to."

She supposed he was right, though it was hardly reassuring. Lily felt sick, every part of her feeling betrayed. Not hurt like she would have expected, though. It turned out any kind of connection she'd had with Matt that could hurt her on a deeper, more personal level had been severed. If not with his death, than with her realizations over the past few weeks and months about the ways in which their relationship had never been healthy. He'd never really seen her, only who he wanted her to be, and it had showed in the way he treated her.

She glanced at Travis, who was still

holding the safe, which he'd closed back up. She looked down at Officer Keller. The bleeding had slowed, it seemed. Maybe the shot had only grazed her, and she'd passed out from shock or pain?

They had to get the information Travis was holding to the police department, or everything they'd endured would be for nothing.

Officer Keller was out of commission. Hopefully Officer Knox would arrive soon and call her an ambulance...

But Lily and Travis still had plays they could make. They were not stuck.

Maybe that was the most amazing realization from this whole ordeal, from her list to her failed relationship with Matt. She realized now that she didn't have to be stuck, and she could change her mind. Her list wasn't foolish or silly, but if she didn't want to pursue it and chase a new dream instead—her eyes went to Travis—then she could do that.

She had options.

And she was going to use one of them now.

Her eyes flickered to Travis again. She angled herself with her back slightly to Matt, so that he wouldn't be able to read her lips. She whispered quietly, "I'm going to run. Get the records to the police."

His eyes widened, and she thought he might have been about to shake his head, but she didn't wait to find out. Instead she stood, sprinted out of the room and yelled, "Timber, come!"

And she was out into the daylight alone.

She didn't have a destination in mind, but she hadn't grabbed her car keys, which limited her options. She hadn't thought through this plan beyond desperately needing to make a way for Travis to get Matt's records to the police.

All but the one she had in her pocket.

Either way, they each had evidence that Matt was a crooked cop.

Her only other thought as she ran was that Lily wanted to keep Travis, herself and Timber safe.

If he'd wanted to, Matt could already have shot Travis and her for the records, she realized now as she sprinted away from her house toward the mountainside trail that she'd run up days ago when all of this had started. Hopefully her running away would throw Matt off enough that he wouldn't shoot Travis but come after her instead.

It might have been a bad plan. But it was the only one she had.

With Timber at her side, she ran up the mountain to where this all began. And where, she hoped, it would end.

With something approaching a happy ending.

SEVENTEEN

The scream of rage that came from Matt as Lily left the room chilled Travis to the core. He'd expected the man to stay and try to get the safe from him, but he ran from the room after Lily.

Glancing down at Officer Keller, Travis hesitated. He hated to leave her defenseless.

At that moment she started to stir. "He shot me? I haven't been shot before." She looked up at Travis, blinked, then looked back down at her arm.

Travis pulled out his phone, dialed 911 and left it with Officer Keller. "I've called 911. They should be here soon, but…"

"Where's Lily?" She seemed to be gaining alertness.

"I've got to go after her." He unlocked the safe, pulled out its contents and shoved them into an inside pocket of his vest. When he ran from the house, he hesitated for a second in the driveway when he saw her car.

Why had he thought she would have driven away? But of course, she may not have had her car keys on her. He glanced down at the ground, willing himself to see footprints or something to indicate where she'd gone, but the ground was grassy and dry.

After a moment's thought, he didn't think he needed any signs like that. The only place he could think that she would have gone was up, back onto the mountain.

Anger and fear coursed through his veins, fear the stronger of the two at the moment. Why had she run somewhere even more isolated? The mountain trails and ridges felt familiar to her, he supposed, but they were familiar to Matt, too. She'd have been better off staying low.

The thought of Matt reaching her intensified Travis's terror. He'd looked almost crazed as he left the room following Lily, and while Travis already knew he was dangerous, this was a different level.

He hadn't been sure how his former friend felt about losing Lily to his faked death, but now Travis wasn't sure he'd considered it correctly. Matt seemed to take Lily's presence for granted, despite the fact that he'd tried to kill her multiple times in the past week. Or had he only been trying to scare her with the gunshots?

It was impossible to say.

Travis hurried up the trail, keeping an

eye out for any sign of Lily, Timber or Matt, but he saw nothing. He was alone.

What-ifs taunted him. Matt could have caught up to Lily already. Then what? Horrible fears taunted him, and he did his best to push them away.

God, be with her, he prayed. As saddened as he'd been when Lily had told him she didn't pray much anymore, he certainly hadn't been praying as much as he usually did. Had he subconsciously picked up a little of that false belief? That God didn't care? Why else wouldn't he talk to God?

As he kept hiking and his lungs and legs burned, he probed his mind for an answer. He only managed to come up with one: he'd just thought he could handle this himself.

After all, he was former law enforcement, capable of taking on this unofficial investigation. And maybe that was right, but even it was, God had given him the gifts to be able to do that. Attempting to do it on his own without God's help and strength? That was a recipe for disaster.

Forgive me, God, he prayed as he hiked. *I want to do this with You. Not alone.* And he meant it.

The morning was chilly, especially since Lily had ditched her vest back at the house. She thought of Officer Keller and hoped she was okay. And Travis...

Surely he understood that she'd run because she wanted this to end, right? She hadn't meant to abandon him, she'd just known they were backed into a corner. Running had been her only thought for what to do.

Although, wasn't that what she'd done in high school, run from Travis?

This was a different situation. She'd like to think of her list as bold and risky, but didn't running away feel safe for her? Her mom had run away. And Lily never wanted to be like that.

Pushing away those uncomfortable thoughts, she kept going. In this case, running seemed to be the right thing. Although she was conscious of the fact that she couldn't run forever. And Matt was probably faster than she was.

Matt. The idea of facing him made her chest tight.

Lily kept running.

When she came to the trail she'd taken only a few days ago, the one that went up to Avalanche Peak itself, she'd stopped and cut left instead, around the ridge to a rocky face of the mountain. She'd come here once during a rainstorm and found some rock formations that had let her hide from the downpour. Was it possible that she might be able to hide from Matt there?

Lily thought it was possible.

Reaching down to pet Timber, Lily

carefully picked her way around the mountainside. Her shoes had decent traction, which was good. A glance to her left confirmed that if she slipped, the scree would likely carry her down several hundred yards. If she didn't crash into a boulder first.

This was definitely a time when balance mattered, so she went slowly. Carefully. Using her hands to help her, she felt her way around one large rock formation, then another. On the third, she didn't think she was going to be able to pass. Her left foot slipped, and she tightened her grip with her hands, closing her eyes against what felt like her inevitable fall.

But she didn't.

Breathing a deep sigh, Lily took a minute to catch her breath and regain her confidence. Her hands and arms were starting to shake now, pumped up with blood. She was exhausted. Had she slept last night? She almost couldn't remember anymore, but yes, she'd slept a bit before she woke up and discovered someone had drugged Timber.

Not just someone, she reminded herself. Matt. *Matt* had drugged Timber. Killed a man. Shot at her.

She never would have believed it without the fingerprints. Why had he left them on the knife? Had he wanted to be caught?

It wouldn't surprise her. It seemed like the kind of power move Matt was capable of. In his mind, he was above the law, so the idea of him taunting them by intentionally leaving fingerprints wasn't entirely surprising.

He'd been so nice when she first met him. Maybe a little controlling. But not like this.

How much of his true personality had he hidden? Was some of it drugs? Could he be taking the drugs he'd been helping to sell, all the while "investigating" the people selling them?

Travis knew Lily was somewhere up the trail along with Timber and Matt, and the knowledge made him creep cautiously upward. He was unwilling to draw attention to himself, unless Lily needed him to do that to keep her safe.

He should have grabbed a gun before he ran out of the house and up the mountainside, but his only thought had been to close the distance between him and Lily. Dumb. Another mistake.

As he climbed, he let his thoughts wander. Mistakes took him back to the police department and his time working there. He considered Matt. Should he have seen that his partner was crooked? It would have been useful.

But realistically could he have?

Now that Lily had mentioned several times over how busy and distracted Matt had been, it was unsurprising that he'd been too involved in the narcotics ring. At the time, though? Travis wasn't sure there was anything he could have done differently. His friend had been in deep cover, and Travis had bought it.

Now, though, the mistakes he'd made on this informal investigation.

This was the other reason Travis had left law enforcement, besides the desire not to be around evil and death so often. Any mistake was high stakes, could hurt someone else. Travis didn't want to live with that kind of stress, yet here he was again. He felt out of control, and he hated that.

Maybe you were never in control in the first place.

The words came across his mind. Like a reminder of something he knew was true. Travis stopped for half a second, then stumbled forward again.

Travis believed in God, believed in the

power of prayer, but he could count on one hand the times he'd had such a clear impression of what God wanted him to know. It made his heart rate rise, and all his senses sharpen. He kept listening, but there were just those two impressions.

He wasn't in control. He needed to give this to God.

He quickened his pace. He had to hurry. Lily needed him. Didn't she?

Like puzzle pieces coming together, Travis saw that maybe that was true. But it was also true that he could only do so much. He wasn't God. He wasn't fully in control of the situation. And God loved Lily more than Travis did.

Travis had been forced to let her go for years. Now that he had her back, everything within him wanted to be the hero she needed.

But maybe Lily didn't need that. Maybe

K-9 Alaskan Defense

she needed God more. And for God to be her ultimate hero.

He blew out a breath, kept up his pace but whispered back, "Okay, God. She's Yours."

And continued on.

God was going to be the hero here, Travis saw that now. But that didn't mean he couldn't do his best, too.

Another crunch on the rocks. Lily's stomach tightened. She didn't think she and Timber were alone on this mountainside anymore. Was it possible Matt had gone on the other trail and was now up above somewhere, unaware of where she was hidden? Or was he lying in wait?

The second wouldn't surprise her. Now that she had a full picture of who he was, nothing about him would surprise her. He probably had never loved her. It hit her hard, somewhere inside where she preferred to think that people were basically good and not capable of this kind of evil.

It made her need for God even more evident. She couldn't believe she'd almost let Matt talk her out of that belief. How had his smooth talking almost made her turn from the beliefs of her childhood? Thank goodness God was forgiving and loving. She had a feeling it wouldn't be the last time she'd need a second chance, but she had full confidence He would always give her one.

Thank You, she whispered in her heart. *Thank You for never leaving me. Even now. You're here, aren't You?*

And He'd given her Timber. It was going to be okay, wasn't it? No matter what?

With tendrils of fear still curling around her, she petted Timber. Tried to breathe in and out. Not long now, and it would be over. Travis may already have delivered the evidence to the police department. Matt was going to be in jail for years, if not forever. Lily just had to hang in there a little while longer.

Carefully, she scooted back even farther.

"Lily. I know you're up here."

Matt's voice was low, almost taunting. She felt herself tense but said nothing in response.

"You were stupid to run, you know. Not that I'm surprised. You've never been very smart, have you?" His laugh was without humor, his voice low. Cold.

She heard more crunching against the rocks. It was still impossible for her to pinpoint where it was coming from. Should she stay where she was, or try to creep farther back into the cave-like formation? Her innate sense of self-preservation told her to move back farther, so she did.

"It's time to let this go. Give me that

paper you took from the safe. Apologize for what you did wrong. Let's start over."

Wait, apologize? Start over?

He was crazy. And she didn't use the word lightly.

"You're nothing by yourself, you know."

It was as though he'd compiled her worst fears, her deepest hurts, and was using them against her as weapons. She supposed he was. *Why* hadn't she seen how unhealthy this relationship was when she'd been in it?

She wasn't alone, though. She wasn't. She dug her fingers deep into Timber's fur.

"Timber, come."

His low voice hadn't diminished in its menacing quality.

The warmth beside Lily evaporated as Timber moved away from her. Moved toward the voice. Toward Matt.

Wait...no.

She wanted to cry out. Had Matt been right? Was it impossible for Timber to switch loyalties? She was a good dog, but she was a dog, after all, unable to reason or understand things like crimes committed, promises broken, lies told.

She was out of sight now.

Lily really was alone.

EIGHTEEN

Panic tightened its grip on her, and Lily struggled against it. It was a lie, she knew that. She was stronger than this. She was not alone.

But without Travis, without her dog, without any clear hope of how she was getting off this mountainside… Lily was afraid this might be the one time when positive thinking wasn't going to help her at all. Was there a time to admit defeat?

She didn't know. Couldn't think anymore.

So with Matt's voice still calling hurtful things, taunting her, she laid her head down in her folded arms and cried.

"Something wrong?" The too-sweet voice chilled her to her core. It echoed at the entrance to her little cave.

She looked up.

Matt looked almost feral, his hair longer than he'd kept it before, somewhat shaggy. His smile was wild, hollow. "You always were exceptionally whiny." He rolled his eyes. "I don't know why I put up with it at all."

His words would have hurt before, but they didn't now. Now Lily felt...fear. Loneliness.

Help, God, she prayed.

"But I did put up with it. Don't forget that." He stepped closer. "And this is how you repay me?"

She wanted to shudder in disgust but held herself still, tensing all her muscles. "You were dead, Matt. We all thought you were dead."

"We. You and my idiot partner? You guys have a thing going on now?"

She didn't want to talk to him about Travis. That relationship was too important, too special to expose to this kind of evil and ridicule. Matt could never understand something like what she and Travis had.

Instead she said nothing. Which seemed to make him even madder.

"And then you have the nerve to try to expose me?" He shook his head. "Don't you know I've already won, Lily?"

She flinched at the sound of her name on his lips. Still didn't reply.

"I see the dog abandoned you," he continued. "She won't be loyal to you, you know."

She heard the implied taunt: no one ever would be.

She'd never specifically told Matt about her mom. She'd never felt close enough to him for that, even when they had been engaged. But somehow he'd picked up on all the vulnerability and sensitivity she had around it. And now he was using it against her.

"It wouldn't do you any good if you did have her," he continued, "because she would never attack me. I was her handler. Her master."

She flinched at the term. "She trusted you," Lily said, hearing her own bitterness creep into her voice.

"You know who I trust? Myself. Maybe the rest of you have to learn that lesson the hard way. Now, you know what's going to happen? You're going to give me the paper you have in your pocket. Then you're going to get out of my way, and I'm going to go find your little boyfriend and get the papers he has."

"There are more up here, aren't there? Papers? You hid things in my house, at the inlet overlook and up here, right?"

He stopped moving toward her and cocked his head to the side as though she was fascinating to him. "Well, you at least figured that much out. I suppose you realized that's why Arnold and I were both up here?"

"Yes." Her voice was still hesitant, but she felt her confidence growing. "I figured he must have decided to reveal that you weren't dead for some reason."

"He didn't want to keep taking the fall for my 'murder.'" Matt sounded disgusted. "As though I wasn't enough of an asset to their organization to make up for that. So he came up here to get the papers, but I figured out what he was up to. He'd been acting strange. I followed him up. Got him out of the picture the day you saw me, then came back another day to find the documents here. Too bad I couldn't get the ones at your house. The fire did more damage overall than I'd counted on, but not enough to easily access the safe."

Everything lined up with what they'd suspected. "Why try to kill me, though?"

Matt shrugged. "I needed you out of the way. If you were dead, getting to the safe was easier. And I knew you'd figure it out eventually, and I didn't want you to turn me in."

As he talked, Lily tried to figure out if there was any way she could escape. He was coming closer and closer to her as he spoke. She could smell his breath now.

She leaned back.

"Something wrong, Lily? You never minded if I was close before."

The reminder disgusted her. The idea of kissing him now was repulsive.

"Wait. Stop. I…" She trailed off. There had to be something else she could ask to slow this down.

"I'm done talking. You're out of chances to get away or whatever you're planning."

Sunlight coming through the caves caught the metal of his gun. He raised it now, bringing it closer to her face. She felt on the ground, grabbed a rock.

"Don't even think about it." Matt brought the gun level with her eyes.

Lily watched in horror as his fingers started to tense.

Then, behind him, Lily saw a flash of something.

Timber!

Her brown body streaked through the air as she launched herself at Matt. She knocked him sideways, and he fired wide. The sound was explosive in the small space, but it didn't hit Lily.

"Timber, no!" Matt yelled, but the German shepherd didn't listen. As though he was the suspect and she was back with the police department working a case, she went after him exactly how she'd been trained. Lily watched in amazement as Timber pinned him to the ground.

Matt struggled against the dog, reaching for his gun.

"No!" She knew if he grabbed the gun now, he wouldn't hesitate to use it on Timber, now that she'd turned into the flesh of his arm with her teeth. Lily couldn't let anything happen to Timber. Instead, she launched herself forward, toward Matt and everything she feared, and grabbed the weapon herself.

"Timber, no!" Matt threw her off, but Timber was not to be deterred. She bit down hard on his arm once again, and he screamed in pain.

"Leave her alone!" Lily screamed, hands on the gun.

"Or what? You'll shoot me? You wouldn't."

"She might not." A new voice echoed through the cave. "But I sure would."

Officer Knox stood in the mouth of the cave, his service pistol drawn.

Travis, looking out of breath, stood beside him.

"Timber, come," Lily commanded.

The German shepherd came to her at once and curled up beside Lily as though to reassure her.

"You wouldn't really have left me, would you?" Lily whispered in her ear, realizing now that Timber must have left to find Matt and stop him from harming Lily. To keep watch, essentially. What an incredible dog.

Timber gladly accepted the scratches behind her ear.

"Matt Davis, you're under arrest for the murder of Arnold Harris. Among other things, I'm sure." Officer Knox's dry voice echoed as he cuffed Matt, whose arm was bleeding from Timber's bite. "You have the right to remain silent…"

"I know the speech," Matt said.

"Yeah. I guess you'd remember that from when you were a cop." Travis looked him up and down. "Pity you didn't remember the part about protecting and serving."

Matt tried to lunge at Travis, but Officer Knox pulled him back.

"That's enough from you." Officer Knox turned to Travis. "Come down later to give a statement?"

Travis nodded.

Officer Knox turned to Lily. "You, too."

"I'll be there," she said with a small smile.

And then Matt and Officer Knox were gone, and it was just Lily and Travis. And, of course, Timber.

"I didn't know if I'd ever see you again," Lily said to Travis with a smile.

"You going to come out of there?" he asked, and when she reached her hand to him, he helped her out. Moving carefully, they walked out of the cave and onto the mountainside.

"I knew I'd see you again," Travis said.

"Oh, yeah?"

"Yeah," he said, stepping closer. "You're strong. I knew you'd be okay."

"You looked a little out of breath and nervous for someone who knew I'd be fine the whole time," she teased, but she was smiling.

"I'm glad you're okay. Do you want to talk?"

"I'm okay, really," she said again.

They stood there together in the morning sunshine, face-to-face.

"I think I was wrong," Travis said finally.

Swallowing hard, Lily stepped back.

He laughed, then pulled her gently forward by her shoulders. "Not about that. Actually, yes, about that. I think

I was wrong that we should just be friends."

It was almost too much, in a good way. God had shown her that He was really all she needed. But that wasn't even all she'd been given. She had Timber. She had friends. And maybe she had Travis as more than that?

Lily waited to hear what he had to say.

"I love you, Lily Peterson," he said at last.

"I love you, too." She barely got the words out before he captured her lips in a kiss.

Maybe Lily wasn't like her mom. Actually, she was sure she wasn't. She didn't have to give up her dreams for love, but neither did she have to give up love for her dreams.

And God was with her, either way. No matter what.

As they stood on the mountainside,

Lily felt contentment flood through her. She didn't need a list.

She had everything she could ever dream of right here.

EPILOGUE

The sun was shining bright on the mountainside when Travis stood with several friends and waited for Lily to walk down the trail that would serve as their aisle. He was amazed by how quickly the year had gone, and how blessed he was.

Was it really only a year ago they'd stood on this mountain before? God had redeemed this place, just like He'd redeemed so many things in their lives.

After they'd sorted out all of the details at the police department, Travis and Lily had talked for the entire night. They talked about the past and the future. And Lily had told him that he meant more to her than any list ever could. Before morning came and Lily drove back to her own home, Travis had told her that one day he wanted to marry her on that mountainside. He'd figured it made sense to make his intentions clear.

Five months later, beside the town's Christmas tree at the lighting festival, he'd asked her to marry him. And she'd said yes.

Now he watched her move toward him, her white dress fitting her perfectly, her hair spilling over her shoulders. She was beautiful. The way she handled difficulty was beautiful. And he loved her.

"We're gathered here today to celebrate the marriage of Travis Beckett and Lily Peterson…"

She faced him there on the trail, and Travis knew every dream he'd ever had had come true. It was funny, they had talked a lot about dreams over the past year, and both of them had come to the conclusion that God's plan was even better than any dreams they could come up with on their own. Even if Travis would have left out some parts of their story, like fearing for Lily's life, he couldn't deny that God was better at being in control than he ever was.

Travis heard little of the pastor's message. He was too distracted by Lily, and with the knowledge that after years apart they'd been given a second chance and would soon be husband and wife.

"You may kiss the bride."

Sharing a smile with Lily, Travis moved forward and kissed her.

And it was even better than he could have dreamed.

* * * * *

*If you liked this story from
Sarah Varland,
check out her previous
Love Inspired Suspense books:*

Alaskan Wilderness Rescue
Alaskan Mountain Search
Alaskan Mountain Attack

*Available now from
Love Inspired Suspense!
Find more great reads at
www.LoveInspired.com.*

Dear Reader,

Thank you for picking up this book! It's because of readers like you that writers get to let our imaginations run wild, and I can't tell you how much I appreciate you.

Lily and Travis were an interesting couple to write about, because they were by all appearances perfect for each other. But Lily let him go years before, essentially because of fear. Due to past experiences in her life, she wasn't convinced she could have a relationship and still pursue her dreams.

It took the events in the story to show her that wasn't true, and that in fact it was possible that she could have even more than she'd dreamed of. I love how true that was in the story, but I love even more how true that is in our lives.

I love to hear from readers! It's fun hearing from people who have read the books and enjoyed them, or from people who have been to Alaska. You can follow me on facebook.com/sarahvarland-author or Instagram @sarahvarland, or send an email to sarahvarland@gmail.com.